"*Pink Slime* is a dystopia all too near to us, in which human connections and sadness over the end matter more than any explanation of the fog and disease that shroud everything. Trías's writing, precise and poetic, turns this beautiful novel into a toxic dream, into a meditation on ruins, bodies, and solitude."

—Mariana Enríquez, author of *Our Share of Night*

"An intimate, melancholic look at an ecologically ravaged future."

—Silvia Moreno-Garcia,
New York Times bestselling author of
Mexican Gothic

"Like a faintly distorting mirror, *Pink Slime* reflects back to us the image of a dying world. In this country, abandoned by God and government, the only consolation is the compassion and silent heroism of a few human beings. With her meticulous prose and the painful lucidity characteristic of her work, Fernanda Trías immerses us in a dystopia that expands around us like a poisonous perfume."

—Guadalupe Nettel, author of *Still Born*,
shortlisted for the 2023 Booker Prize

"Like a nightmare, like an omen, like the lines of an exquisite poem, *Pink Slime* echoes in my memory long after I read it. A book has never been so relevant, necessary, painful, and simply splendid."

—Jazmina Barrera, author of *Cross-Stitch*

"A beautiful elegiac meditation on parenting—in this case, the deep connection between a mother and son."

—*Locus*

"This is not a dystopia, but a full-on, technicolor apocalypse. . . . That we are in the company of someone who truly cares makes the horror all the more visceral."

—*The Scotsman*

"Powerful and beautifully written, this is a disturbing read, depicting a terrifyingly convincing near-future scenario. The reader shares the achingly sad narrator's feelings as caregiver, daughter, and ex-lover."

—*The Guardian*

"Trías expertly encapsulates the relationship between mother and child, obligation and affection, and the conflation of fear with love."

—*Kill Your Darlings*

"Latin American fantastika is in the midst of a remarkable renaissance. The latest of this string of exhilarating new books to find its way into English is Uruguayan novelist Fernanda Trías's *Pink Slime*."

—*The Saturday Paper*

"It's a dystopic work worthy of J. G. Ballard, where even in hopelessness there remains a flickering shard of hope or resignation."

—*The Irish Times*

"Precise, luminous, and powerful."

—*L'Indipendente*

"Fernanda Trías revisits the apocalyptic novel with subtlety and intelligence; not as a heroic epic of survival, but through intense emotions and a choice that must be made."

—*LH le magazine*

"[In this] novel—which belongs to that category of books that don't leave you once you've finished reading but rather force you to think of them, to keep returning to them—the stubbornness upon which we all depend in order to save ourselves, those we love, and our environment begins to emerge."

—*La Stampa*

"After Samanta Schweblin's *Fever Dream* and Mariana Enríquez's *Our Share of Night*, *Pink Slime* by Fernanda Trías completes a triptych of extraordinary works that have come to us in the last decade from the Rio de la Plata area. Three very different novels that nonetheless share the force with which they look straight into the abyss, maintaining the lucidity necessary to focus on each revealing detail."

—*L'Indice*

"Intoxicating."

—*Lire*

"*Pink Slime*, like all truly great novels, etches itself indelibly onto the sensitive plate of one's mind."

—*Transfuge*

pink slime

A NOVEL

FERNANDA TRÍAS

translated by HEATHER CLEARY

SCRIBNER

New York • Amsterdam/Antwerp • London • Toronto • Sydney/Melbourne • New Delhi

SCRIBNER
An Imprint of Simon & Schuster, LLC
1230 Avenue of the Americas
New York, NY 10020

This book has been selected to receive financial assistance from English PEN's
PEN Translates programme, supported by Arts Council England.
English PEN exists to promote literature and our understanding of it, to uphold
writers' freedoms around the world, to campaign against the persecution
and imprisonment of writers for stating their views, and to promote
the friendly co-operation of writers and the free exchange of ideas.
www.englishpen.org

Supported using public funding by
**ARTS COUNCIL
ENGLAND**

For Rita,
For Santi and Mónica,
For Mia Joyce.

And this points to the difference between the one-dimensional line and the two-dimensional surface: the one aims at getting somewhere; the other is there already, but may reveal how it got there. This difference is one of temporality, and involves the present, the past, and the future.

"LINE AND SURFACE"
VILÉM FLUSSER (TRANSLATED BY ERIK EISEL)

I am divided from myself by the distance I find myself in,
the one who is dead is divided from death by a great distance.
I plan to cross this distance, resting along the way.
Face up, in the dwelling of desire,
stock still, in my place—opposite the locked door,
with a winter's light at my side.

IMMANENT VISITOR
JAIME SÁENZ (TRANSLATED BY FORREST GANDER AND KENT JOHNSON)

pink slime

Why did you try to become a saint?
Why not?
Why did you try to bite me?
Because you let me.

When the fog rolled in, the port turned into a swamp. Shadows fell across the plaza, filtering between the trees and leaving the long marks of their fingers on all they touched. Under each unbroken surface, mold cleaved silent through wood, rust bored into metal. Everything was rotting. We were, too. If I didn't have Mauro, I'd spend all day wandering around, guided through the fog by the neon sign flickering in the distance: PAL CE HOTE . The missing letters hadn't changed, though it wasn't a hotel anymore; like so many other buildings in the city, it had been taken over by squatters. What day was that? Sometimes I can still hear the neon, its electric hum and the crackle of another letter on the verge of shorting out. The squatters kept the sign lit, but not out of laziness or nostalgia. They did it to remind themselves they were alive. That they could still do something arbitrary, something purely aesthetic. That they could still transform the landscape.

If I'm going to tell this story I should choose a starting point, begin somewhere. But where? I was never any good with beginnings. The day I saw the fish? Certain details leave their mark on time and render a moment unforgettable. It was cold, and the fog condensed into droplets on the overflowing dumpsters. I don't know where all that garbage came from. It seemed to consume and excrete itself. And how do you know *we're* not the waste? Max might have said something like that. I remember turning at the old corner store, with its windows boarded over, and how the greenish-red light of the hotel sign washed over me as I stepped onto the rambla.

Mauro would be back the next day, bringing with him another month of confinement and work. Cooking, cleaning, monitoring his every movement. Each time they came to collect him I spent a whole day catching up on the sleep he threatened or interrupted. This endless vigil was the reason Mauro's parents paid me the exorbitant salary they knew would never compensate me. Breathing in the stale air of the port, prowling the streets, visiting my mother or Max—these were the luxuries I afforded myself on the days my time didn't carry a price. If I was lucky, that is, and there was no wind.

The only people on the rambla were fishermen with the collars of their jackets pulled up around their ears, their hands red and cracked. The water stretched wide in all directions, an estuary where the river became a shoreless sea. The fog blurred the horizon. It was ten o'clock or eleven or three under that flat, milky light. The algae floated nearby like bloodshot phlegm, but the fishermen seemed not to care. They rested their buckets next to their beach chairs, baited their hooks, and gathered the strength of their brittle arms to cast their lines as far as they could. I liked the sound of the reels spooling out: it reminded me of summers spent riding my bicycle in San Felipe, no brakes, knees angled high to avoid the pedals. That bicycle contained my whole childhood, just like those beaches that would later be cordoned off with yellow tape the wind would periodically destroy and a few policemen in face masks would rehang. KEEP OUT, it said. Why? You'd have to be crazy to want to go like that: infected, exposed to a nameless disease that didn't even promise a speedy death.

Once, long before I married Max, I saw fog as dense as it was that day. It was in San Felipe, just before dawn, sometime in early December. I remember because the beach town was still empty, except for the few of us who had been summering there all our lives. Max and I walked slowly along the road, not looking at the black sand of the beach, accustomed to the rhythm of the breaking waves. That sound was like a watch to us, a certainty of all the summers to come. Unlike the tourists, we didn't go to San Felipe to get away from it all. We went there to affirm the continuity of something. It was pitch-dark except for Max's flashlight, but we knew the way. We stopped near the lookout, where lovers often hid, and leaned over the white wooden banisters. Max pointed his flashlight at the beach and through the fog we saw a swarming mass of crabs. The sand seemed to breathe, to swell like a sleeping beast. The crabs gleamed in their halo of light, they gushed from cracks in the boardwalk. Hundreds of them, tiny. What did Max say? I don't remember. I think we were both shaken, as if we had just been alerted to the existence of something incomprehensible, something bigger than ourselves.

In winter along the rambla, though, there was no sign of so much as a mullet. The fishermen's buckets were empty, their bait waiting useless in plastic bags. I sat down near a man wearing a Russian-style hat with earflaps. My hands trembled from the cold, but I didn't do anything to still them. Unlike Max, I didn't view a person's will as independent from their body. This belief had led him to dedicate the last few years to extravagant experiments: purges, privations, weights hooked through his skin. The ecstasy of pain. The fasting organism is a single vast membrane, he would say, a thirsty plant left too long in the dark. Maybe. But Max was after something else: to separate himself from his body, that indomitable desire-generating machine, which knew neither conscience nor limits—repugnant but also innocent, pure.

The fisherman sensed I was looking at him. With my feet dangling over the water, my maskless face, and my backpack, which seemed to be loaded with stones, he must have thought I was another lost soul ready to jump into the river. Maybe my whole family was dead, admitted one by one to the critical care wing at Clinics, never to emerge. The water barely made a sound as it lapped against the seawall and the air was completely still. How long could this calm last? Every war had its cease-fires, even this one we fought unarmed.

The line suddenly tensed, and I watched the fisherman cinch and reel in until a small fish popped into the air. It arched weakly, but the glint off its silvery scales brought a smile to the man's face. He grabbed it with his gloveless hand and removed the hook. No one could know what death and what miracle that animal held within it, and the two of us admired it accordingly. I expected the man to drop it into his bucket, even if just for a little while, but he threw it back immediately. It was so slight that it made no noise as it broke the surface. The last fish. One minute later and it would be far away, immune to the dense seaweed, to the death trap of algae and waste. The man turned to look at me, gesturing with his hand.

This is the starting point I choose for my story, its false beginning. I could easily make an omen of it, justify it as a sign of things to come, but I won't. That's all: an hour like any other on a day like any other, except for the fish that soared through the air and fell back into the water.

Once upon a time.

There was what?

Once upon a time there was a time.

That never was?

That never again.

The few taxis along the rambla drove slowly with their windows up. They were trolling for an emergency, for some poor creature who'd just collapsed in the middle of the street and needed to be dropped off at Clinics. It was worth the risk: the Ministry of Health paid the fare plus a contaminant fee. I tried to wave one down; it honked at me but kept going. I removed my backpack and rested it on the ground. It was full of books. The epidemic had given us back what we'd thought was lost forever: a country of readers nestled far from the sea, the wealthy in their hilltop estates or mansions, the poor overflowing the small cities we used to mock for being empty, lacking, dim.

Two more taxis passed before I had any luck. As soon as the driver greeted me, I could tell he was one of those who never miss a chance to show you how streetwise they are.

'You'll draw attention with that backpack,' he said.

'They won't find much inside.'

I set the backpack on the seat beside me and gave him my mother's address. Through the window I caught a glimpse of the Masonic temple across the avenue, blurred by a grimy curtain of fog.

'Los Pozos. You live out there?'

'I'm visiting someone.'

He bragged that he knew Los Pozos like the back of his hand because he'd spent his childhood at his grandmother's house there. I told him I knew it, too, but that was a lie. After the evacuation, my mother had decided to move into one of the neighborhood's abandoned mansions. The owners, with that special pride of aristocrats who have fallen on hard times, were renting them out for a song to keep life flowing through them. They wanted to keep their elegant gardens pruned, their meticulously draped windows unboarded, their bedrooms free of drifters. It was this gilded past that gave my mother a sense of security, not the distance she'd put between herself and the algae. My mother had a blind faith in sturdy materials and might even have believed that the contamination couldn't pass through a good wall, solid and silent, or a well-constructed roof with no cracks for the wind to sneak into. The contamination wasn't as bad in the inland streams as it was along the coastline, but a horrible stench of garbage, silt, and chemicals permeated the neighborhood.

As we were about to pull up to the house, we saw someone rummaging around in a dumpster.

'You see? It's them who'll rob you,' said the taxi driver. 'They don't give a damn about the red wind, or about any damn thing.'

The man's legs wriggled like an insect's as he tried not to fall headfirst into the trash. The fog wasn't any thinner; sheltered from the wind, Los Pozos was even more of a swamp. It was as if the clouds formed there, exhaled by the earth itself, and you could feel the moisture on your face, as slow and cold as a slug's trail.

'You know what I call the people who live out here?' the driver asked.

'What?'

'*Kindasortas*. Kinda crazy, but also sorta not.' He laughed. 'Tell me I'm wrong.'

I opened the front gate and headed straight for the garden. Why bother announcing my arrival? If she wasn't there, she was probably visiting the schoolteacher, who had refused to leave town because she didn't want to abandon her grand piano. They spent hours like that: my mother reading and the schoolteacher playing something sublime, or pretending she was. Sometimes other old people from the area would join them, and my mother and the schoolteacher would play hostess in a city in ruins. Their guests would ask my mother for reading recommendations and she'd talk about the characters in books as if they lived in the neighborhood: oh, but what do you expect from him; steer clear of her, she's a live one; oh, that dear woman; that poor devil.

I found my mother in the garden with her feet sunk into a flower bed, pruning the plants with a large pair of shears. The crunch of my steps alerted her to my presence; when she saw me, she removed one of her gloves, which were filthy and too big for her.

'Come look at this,' she said.

She showed me the new buds on the plants. She saw them as a miracle, as life triumphing over this death of acid and darkness. I told her there were more animals than ever in Chernobyl; even species that had been endangered before were reproducing in the absence of humans. My mother didn't see the irony—she took it as yet another triumph of life over death.

'*Human*, Mom. Over human death.'

'Details,' she said, and gestured toward the kitchen door. 'Are you hungry? I made scones.'

On the marble counter I found bread, cheese, orange marmalade, and even an avocado. Probably better not to ask where she got the avocado. A white cloth was draped over the scones. It was like a feast. With Mauro, I inhaled a few bites whenever I could; eating when my body asked for food had become a foreign concept, an impulse I'd learned to ignore. I needed to forget my own needs, to synchronize my hunger with Mauro's or wolf something down while he slept to avoid another tantrum. Tricks, strategies I'd learned over the months.

I put everything on a tray and went back out to the garden.

'We should make the most of this reprieve,' I said as I set the clinking tray on a glass table with lightly rusted iron legs.

Two scones, butter, marmalade, a cup of tea, cutlery specific to each task. I strained to hide my joy at these banalities: separating the scone with my fingers and hearing the dry crack as it broke in half; slicing thin pats of butter with a round-tipped knife that looked like a toy; stirring my tea with a silver spoon that weighed more in my hand than all my spoons combined. The luxuries only a disaster could have afforded us. We were taking tea in a garden in Los Pozos, the fog swirling around us like strips of chiffon.

'You cut your hair,' said my mother. 'And it's curlier now.'

'The humidity does that.'

'It looked better long. Shinier. You look more alive with long hair.'

'I like it this way.'

'Just doing my job,' she replied with a shrug. 'If your own mother doesn't tell you these things . . .'

'You're honest, I'll give you that.'

'Better to be honest than cynical, dear. Candor is a virtue in times like these. Besides, I'm only talking about your hair. Hair grows, doesn't it?'

She gazed off into the distance, toward the garden of the house next door, with its shutters closed and black holes in the roof where tiles were missing. Other houses behind it, blurred by the fog, were boarded up and eaten away by neglect and by the gases in the air.

'Resignation is not a virtue,' she said. 'You have to fight for what you want.'

'Tell me something, Mom. Why are you still here?'

On the table, her gardening gloves looked like the amputated hands of a giant.

'I could ask you the same thing. What are you trying to prove? That you were hurt so badly you don't care anymore whether you live or die?'

'Max has nothing to do with this.'

'Have you heard from him? What's he up to these days? You can tell me.'

'No, not a word.'

'You did what you could,' she sighed. 'But that marriage was cursed.'

'Cursed? And do you remember who cursed it from the start?'

She leaned over, eyes on the ground between her feet, and propped her elbows on the edge of the table to cradle her head in her hands. Her curls fell forward, covering her face. It's too much, I heard her say. It's too much. I steadied myself for the biting comment, for the words that would cut me right to the bone, but this time she said nothing. She just stayed that way, offering me the gray roots at the crown of her head. It was as if we spoke different languages, and neither was able to learn the other's. I'd spent my whole life studying her movements, her expressions, trying to interpret what I'd thought was a secret code. The memory of that swarm of crabs came rushing back. My mother inspired the same primitive fear in me, the same foreboding, and right then I longed for the comfortable way we'd hated each other before.

'Mom . . .' I slid my fingers into her frizzy curls until they reached her rough, swollen knuckles. It was far more physical contact than we'd allowed ourselves in years. 'It doesn't matter.'

She looked up. The blood had rushed to her face.

'I know,' she said. 'What's the difference?'

She stood and grabbed the plate, where only a few yellow crumbs remained, then went to the kitchen and came back with more scones. I devoured them so quickly I couldn't help but think of Mauro. I told my mother about the time I forgot to take out the trash and woke up in the middle of the night to the sound of mice. The kitchen light was on and from the doorway I saw Mauro in his underwear with the bag in tatters all around him. He'd been going through the garbage and sticking everything—edible or not—in his mouth, including a hamburger wrapper made of aluminum foil. The foil gave him a shock when he bit down and he spit it out angrily, chewed up like a piece of gum.

'He always comes back like that. I don't know why they take him.'

The moisture was beginning to seep through my pants, despite the hard, thin cushion that covered the iron chair. I wrapped my hands around the teacup and let the steam warm my face.

'Poor thing,' said my mother, meaning something else. I saw the
fear in her eyes, her terror as she imagined me at home near the
port, exposed to the red wind, living alongside the disease. She never
would have guessed I'd be capable of something like that.

'How much longer until you've saved up enough?'

There it was. The question. She'd been biting her tongue, waiting for the right moment.

'I don't know. A few months, maybe a year. I'm fine here.'

'You're at risk.'

'So are you.'

She clicked her tongue.

'I've lived my life.'

The crisis had ended up smoothing things over between us. Not
long ago, we could barely spend five minutes together. Her double-
edged questions, her benevolent campaigns to control my life. You
can't wish so intensely for someone else's well-being. It's monstrous;
aggressive, even. A year earlier, any comment about Max would have
sent me storming out of the house. But like the wind unearthing dry,
scattered bones, the epidemic had brought us closer—if only on that
barren terrain.

I lied to her anyway. I already had enough money to leave, more
than anyone else in the port. I had so much that I could've made
sandwiches of cash, fed Mauro paper lettuce. But, like the fishermen, I couldn't imagine myself anywhere else.

'I didn't come here to talk about that. Tell me about you. How's
it going out here, where the other half lives?' I asked, attempting a
joke.

She launched into local gossip. The schoolteacher was having an affair with an agronomist who, after the red wind ravaged the livestock, had gone from absolute nobody to coveted specialist, a self-appointed expert in legumes. On top of that, he was an investor in the new meat-processing plant and in real estate developments further inland. He only went to the city to recruit desperate souls from around the port and other neighborhoods for cheap labor, piling them into trucks and driving back with them.

'She's head over heels for him,' said my mother with a dismissive little wave. She saw herself as immune to those passions. 'Don't care for the man, myself. Clammy skin.'

My mother's face bunched in grotesque folds when she laughed: one eye closed tighter than the other and the excess skin of her cheeks rolled back, revealing the metal between her teeth. Time did that to faces, and this change was only a superficial reminder of what was happening in the unseen parts of us. She looked relaxed now, carefree. Her fingers were stiff with arthritis, the veins on her hands blue and bulging. We both took the calcium pills and the vitamin D recommended by the Ministry of Health, but no one knew how long we had before we began to snap like dry branches. She gathered the crumbs from the scones with her fingertips and let them fall onto the plate. It did me good to get out of my own head for a while, to escape the circular thoughts I'd once called *my fixation*. My mother saw Max as a weakling who'd opted out of life because he couldn't handle it. She thought I should turn the page, relegate him to the undesirable yet dignified oblivion of the past. And Max? How did he see her? Probably as a necessary evil, an opportunity to practice compassion. He would have been completely untroubled by the arrogance of this stance. At the end of the day, Max and my mother were enemies at war over a minuscule territory.

'And Valdivia has a cough. They took him to Clinics and he spent the whole day there, but then they sent him home.'

Ramón Valdivia owned the only store in Los Pozos, which had become our connection to the thriving inland towns. He was like a link in some chain pulled taut between us, on one side, and life on the other.

'It must be the flu,' I said. 'The man never rests.'

'And he has two little grandchildren inland, from his youngest daughter. He supports them all.'

'They just keep having babies out there, don't they?'

Business had gotten worse for Valdivia. Not only because of illegal competition, street vendors setting up their carts under every window, but also because people kept migrating further in. Something would give them a scare: a relative sent to the quarantine wing at Clinics, an alarm catching them far from home. In other words, they'd suddenly develop a concrete sense, rather than an abstract idea, of the relentless advance of the red wind. Unless you've lived it, you could never imagine the nauseating stench, the sudden heat, the river swelling like an octopus, the foam tinted crimson by algae. From one moment to the next, the landscape was transformed: the alarm's deafening blare, hands emerging from buildings to pull windows shut, fishermen packing up their things. The inlanders watched the phenomenon on television, saw the case numbers rise, and worried all those people might flock to their clean, safe cities.

'And when does the little one come back?'

'Tomorrow. They're dropping him off at noon.'

'Poor thing . . . children need their mothers.'

'He's fine with me.'

'It's not the same.'

'Sometimes it's better.'

'It's never the same.'

This was new. A few years earlier, when I was nearing forty and my marriage was falling apart, my mother had abandoned her life-long stance on the matter and had begun preaching the sanctity of motherhood.

'Well,' she said, 'you'd better get going. The alarm could sound at any minute.'

'We've had fog for days.'

'Don't push your luck.'

I pulled the books from my backpack and made an unsteady tower of them on the garden table.

'Let the record show that they all made it back,' I said.

She peered at their spines, some of which were torn and illegible, her finger moving like one of those rods used for finding water underground.

'I made you a little pile in there,' she said.

Then she'll go inside to call a taxi; when she returns, she'll be carrying the last scones wrapped in a paper towel and a stack of four or five books.

'Your taxi's on the way.'

I'll stick the books in my backpack and the scones in my coat pocket, where I'll find the crumbs of visits past. My mother will walk me to the door, and we'll say goodbye with a quick hug.

'Take good care of yourself.'

'You too. The scones turned out well.'

My next driver was the religious type, with images of the Virgin Mary everywhere and the radio tuned to a Christian station. Even so, he made sure the taxi's windows were closed tight. There was a limit to his faith.

'You ever see one of the infected?' he asked.

'Have you?'

'It's like they're being . . . skinned alive. The other day I had to drive one. Left the seat full of flakes, like dandruff, you know? Dry, white, sort of transparent. The wind peels them right down to the muscle.'

'People say all kinds of things.'

'Sure, but this I saw with my own eyes.'

We drove on in silence. I focused on blocking out the images. As long as I avoided picturing Max affected by the disease, my superstitions told me, nothing bad could happen to him. To distract myself, I thought about Mauro and what I still needed to do before he arrived. Right then, he was probably at the family estate munching on grass and flowers with red splotches on his cheeks, which weren't used to sunlight. In the afternoon, some ranch hand would take him for a horse ride. They'd feed him whatever he wanted all weekend, and then I'd have to deal with his hunger and his tantrums. In less than twenty-four hours, either his father or his mother (never the two together) would leave him on my doorstep a few pounds heavier. Having purged their guilt for the month, they'd give him back to me like a customer returning an unsatisfactory product.

I let Mauro gain ground, let him expand in my mind like a hot-air balloon so I wouldn't have to see Max flayed alive, his skin cracked open to the muscle. I clutched the backpack on my lap. I never told my mother, and now could never tell her, that I wasn't going to read her books, that at most I'd skim them so I could stammer a few more or less coherent things when she asked me about them.

'Imagine dying like that,' the taxi driver said. 'Your nerves all exposed . . . Everything so . . . what's the word?'

'Raw?'

'They even had to disinfect my taxi. May God have mercy on his soul.'

He sighed this last part, maybe a little ashamed. He had been slow to think of his god.

Imagine you met me today.

Impossible.

Just imagine.

Where do we meet?

Somewhere absurd.

A mattress store.

Imagine we met in a mattress store.

I'm buying a mattress and you . . .

We're both buying mattresses.

A showroom, one of those places with mattresses wrapped in plastic.

And tube lights.

We sit down on the same mattress. It's queen size, but cheap.

You bounce a little.

And what happens next?

We both lie back.

We're testing it.

We stare at the tube lights going *tzzzzzz*.

Two strangers.

But you turn and look at me.

Me? Okay, fine.

I turn, too, and for a moment we look at each other.

There.

On the plastic-wrapped mattress.

And then?

Just imagine it had been like that.

My mother was right. Clinics was in a state of collapse. I waited in line for fifteen minutes to reach the front desk; while the receptionist looked for Max's name in her register, my fear took on the physical form of a stone. That patient is no longer here, she could have said with a steady voice. Maybe they were trained that way. Maybe any clerk whose job involved announcing deaths had to take an intensive course where they learned to repeat the same phrase naturally, efficiently. We're sorry, that name is not in our records. A tidy inventory of death, a way to turn it into a pair of socks or shoes: we don't have, we can't find, we're all out.

But this time he was, at least he still was, and the receptionist handed over my blue card. I'd spent 280 minutes with Max over the past year, not counting the first two months, when they'd kept him in the quarantine wing. What would happen if I tried to stay past my appointed half hour? I'd never considered it and wasn't sure it was something I even wanted to do. For what? To see him like that a little longer, supine and gaunt, his skin loose, yellowed? The half-hour limit made us all feel better, the ones who left and the ones who stayed. Come to think of it, that rule was the new Ministry's only compassionate act.

How old were we when we saw those crabs? Eighteen, nineteen maybe. We'd always pretended to be older than we were. We wanted to speed up time, become adults, because we thought that life began then, that what we were living was just practice. Max and I didn't have a beginning. But everything starts somewhere, doesn't it? No. Summer would arrive, and I knew Max would be waiting for me in San Felipe; it never crossed my mind that he might not be there, or that at some point he hadn't been. It was like . . . like what? We know everything is made of atoms and that atoms aren't solid; they're holes with electrons spinning around a nucleus at full speed. But we see something else. A table. A lamp. A pot. That's the kind of thing Max and I would talk about as we sat on the dunes, digging for shells. If only we could see it, Max said, everything in motion, spinning and spinning. And you, I said. You'd be spinning, too, it would be like you had no eyes or arms or legs. Just imagine.

I took one of the elevators that had been reserved for the epidemic. It was so crowded inside I had to press myself against the wall to make room for another terrified face. I was surrounded by two kinds of faces: terrified ones and ones lifeless as marble. It wasn't that the lifeless faces had conquered fear, they had just run out of room for it. The door didn't close; too many bodies pressed against the sensor. A voice gave an order and the bodies crushed nervously together. Every minute counted and each card was a treasured object, never to be folded or stained. If your card got creased, you had to go to Forms and Documents and then wait weeks, or even months, for a new one. No one was allowed to visit a patient without a card.

There was no mirror in the elevator, which was a relief. Max wasn't the only one who'd aged—I was pale and had dark circles under my eyes. They say people stay the age they were when we first met them. It's not true. I watched Max grow up, heard his voice change. And then I watched him dry out like a branch, watched his abdomen cave in from fasting, his nails yellow from tobacco, the first gray hairs appear in his beard. How he saw me, if he saw me at all, I had no idea. People who knew Max thought he looked past the surface of things. At first, it made them uncomfortable; then they were flattered by the way his eyes locked onto them. But I know he wasn't looking deep inside them, into that inaccessible part of the other. He was looking through them, as if they stood between him and what he desired, which was always somewhere else.

When the doors opened on ten, I needed to push my way through the crowd. I was the only one getting off on that floor, again. As I muttered 'excuse me,' I could feel the silence expand. It seemed like admiration, but it was the silence of envy. Everyone wanted to be among the chosen few who made it out of the critical care wing (a place that was more a time than a physical space) and were transferred to the wing for the chronically ill. Exceptions, maybe even miracles.

'Excuse me,' I said. 'Excuse me,' among grumbled protests.

The receptionist had the radio on low: white noise to mask the groans of the patients and the occasional laughter of relatives. I told her I was there for room 1024 and she asked for my card. While she carefully wrote down my name and time of arrival, I looked at the sign behind her: CHRONIC CARE. That's where the statistical improbabilities slept, the ones who couldn't manage to get better or lose ground. Maybe that's what stoicism gave Max: the ability to stay alive by virtue of incredulity or indifference. According to the Ministry, all the infected were equals (*Every life is unique*, the new slogan claimed), but the doctors wanted the chronic patients alive more than the criticals or the patients in quarantine. The chronics carried inside them the secret of the algae.

The woman returned my card and waved me on. I walked down the polished hallway to room 1024. The door was ajar, and I could hear voices on the other side. I leaned toward the crack and saw a nurse arranging Max's blankets. He said something I couldn't quite make out, and she laughed, rocking back on the heels of her black shoes. You and your addiction to people-pleasing, I thought, but a part of me understood that he was dying and therefore immune to criticism. I lingered in the hallway, even though it meant wasting minutes. I studied the nurse's movements, her smile, the way she rested one hand on the blanket, right at Max's knee, as if she'd left it there by accident. She was young, I guessed from where I stood. She might still be holding on to the illusion of a future, of the possibility of building one with him. She had no idea, how could she, what it was like to be connected to Max by an elastic band that shot you toward him with the same force you exerted trying to get away. It didn't matter how long it had been since the last time I saw him, how great that distance was, because the elastic always held me in the painful, quivering tension of my inevitable return. On her way out, the nurse told me Max was doing better than the both of us combined. She couldn't have been even twenty years old; up close, she looked like a little girl wearing a costume. Her smock was two sizes too big and covered her knees.

Max shared a room with two other chronics. When I entered, they were both either sleeping, sedated, or sick of bearing such high hopes. Max hugged me, and I took the opportunity to sniff his neck, which smelled faintly of tobacco.

'How long did it take you to convince her?' I asked.

'Who?'

'You're smoking. Isn't she worried about your lungs? Or does she think you're immune to that, too?'

'I don't know. How did I convince you?'

He stretched out his hand and we laced our fingers together. He looked me over slowly, studying me, and I felt the familiar weight of a gaze that came from far away, like light reaching me from a dead star. He asked how things were at the agency and I was suddenly all too aware that he was only pretending to be himself, putting up a kind of facade to protect the world from his absence.

'Are you still writing for that little magazine?' he asked. 'What was it called? *The Good Lie*?'

'*The Good Life*,' I said. 'And no, I quit the agency decades ago. I look after Mauro now, remember?'

'The fat kid you left me for?'

'Don't tease, Max.'

'Fine, all right. You didn't leave me for him, you left me on my own merits.' Suddenly, he was himself again, as if he'd remembered over those few minutes. 'He *is* fat, though, isn't he?'

'Don't say that.'

'What did I say? The Universe is truth.'

'Yeah, yeah. The Universe is the truth.'

'*Truth*. Not *the* truth, as if there were only one.'

I looked out the window. The dingy fog blocked the view of the buildings across the way.

'You want to know the truth, Max? You're unbearable.'

'That's one truth,' he said, laughing.

We fell silent. He didn't keep going, and I didn't look at the clock. When our time ran out, the young nurse would let us know.

'Why did you go outside, if the alarm was sounding? Explain it to me.'

Max looked at his feet, a ridge interrupting the blanket's tightness.

'You're not going to sit?' he asked, gesturing toward the visitor's couch, a squat ottoman draped in a removable slipcover that looked like a sheet.

'Tell me. Tell me why you didn't care about the wind.'

'The wind? Is it the wind you mean? Or are you asking me why I didn't care about you?'

We stared at each other and neither softened our gaze until I sat on the visitor's couch. I waited for him to say something else. He was waiting, too, and the silence dragged on. I noticed a metallic taste in my mouth: my gums were bleeding again. The patient in the bed closest to Max turned his head toward us. It seemed like he might wake up, but he just let out a snort, licked his lips, and went back to lying motionless. Max didn't even look at him.

'You keep coming to see me because you're full of rage,' he said.

'That's one truth.'

'And the other?'

'I had the afternoon off.'

Just then, there was a noise at the door. The young nurse entered with a tray.

'Don't worry,' she said, 'you still have time. I'm just here to change his drip.'

She walked over to the third patient, whose bed was near the far wall, and performed a maneuver with his plastic IV bag. I looked quizzically at Max. Patients in chronic care didn't receive medication or therapy. He made a gesture as if to say, It's a long story.

'Patricio refuses to eat,' he said. 'He wants out of this room, even if it's by the back door.'

The nurse just smiled.

'It's understandable. Wanting to get out of here, I mean.'

'It's selfish,' she corrected me. 'Many people would give everything they have to be in his position.'

She finished hooking up the IV and checked her watch. She wasn't pretty, aside from the plump indifference of her youth.

'I'll leave you two alone so you can say goodbye.'

She didn't close the door all the way when she left. Max gestured me toward him. I climbed onto the right side of his bed, where there was more room, and rested my head on his shoulder. He was so tall he barely fit in that little hospital bed sitting up. We lay there for a while in silence, which in that room meant the faint purr of breathing and machines in the distance. When I closed my eyes, the light coming in through the window painted a green rectangle inside my eyelids. The rectangle began filling with shadows and in one of those shadows I saw Max. I saw the sea, choppy and gray, waves breaking erratically. They didn't crest but slid across the surface like rollers loaded with white paint. There would be a sunset; the horizon was clear. The sand was wet, its chill soaked into my feet, and the wind sliced through our clothes like the furious beating of a bird's wings. Max, or the shape of Max, walked toward the shore, dark against the sand and tall at first, then shorter and shorter as the water ate its way up his legs. I watched him step into the churning, dirty foam. The cold didn't bother him; it never had. The sun had passed the strip of clouds and was now a huge, blinding disc. The waves crashed against the shadow, eating away its torso and then its shoulders, until it was only a head bobbing in and out of the water. Black dot, red sun, shattered white foam.

Something moved. Max. The metal of the bed creaked. I opened my eyes and searched in vain for something in the rectangle of the window.

'What did the Buddhist monk say to his son?' he asked.

'I don't know, what?'

'One day, my boy, all this Nothing will be yours.'

The stale waft of his breath reached me just as the nurse stuck her head in again to announce that it was time for the visitors to leave. She said 'visitors,' plural, like I wasn't the only one. While I put on my coat and backpack, I could see her white figure waiting stiff in the doorway.

'Where'd they train this one?' I whispered.

Max raised his shoulders and the left corner of his mouth, an expression I'd known since we were kids. The elastic connecting us pulled taut; in the weeks to come, as the days with Mauro multiplied, it would stretch as far as it could before launching me right back at him.

'What can I say?' he replied. 'We're martyrs for the nation.'

Tell me.

What?

What's that paradox about how you can't surrender without first
 letting go, but letting go is impossible until you've surrendered?

The beginning is never the beginning. What we often mistake for the beginning is just the moment we realize something has changed. One day, the fish appeared; that was one beginning. We woke up to find the beaches covered with silvery fish, like a carpet made of bottle caps or shards of glass. The light glinting off them was painfully intense. The Ministry sent the garbagemen to clean it up. The fish weren't even flapping around; they'd been stiff a while already, since even before the water tossed them out. The men came armed with shovels and rakes, but not with face masks. They spent the whole day piling fish, one shovelful at a time, into glittering pyramids on the sand. The sun was still bright in the afternoon sky. That other thing that would begin, hadn't yet. The pyramids looked like mirages, shimmering in the glare. Later, the army arrived; the soldiers gathered the fish into huge nets and attached the sides to a truck. They took them away. They didn't say where to.

I was on my way back from Clinics when the alarm sounded. The taxi driver didn't speed up; he was a skeptic. Steeped in conspiracy theories, he said the whole thing was a lie made up by the State.

'So you'd swim at Martínez Beach?'

'No,' he said, 'but I never would've. When I was little, my brother caught something on that beach, paralyzed him. And how many years ago was that. Left him one leg shorter than the other, and I can't say for a fact that's what gave him diabetes, but he's got diabetes. I'm talking sixty years ago now. More than half a century, they've been cooking up this line about the algae.'

'You've never seen one of the infected?'

'Listen. Some people, they don't have a disease, so they make one up. One time I got this guy, he was screaming bloody murder. Staring at his hands, his arms, and just screaming. I took a good look and I didn't see anything wrong with him, except that his skin was red from all that yelling.'

'Then what happened?'

'The Ministry gave me a little ticket for me to get my car decontaminated, but I never went. Waste of time. And look at me, here to tell the tale. What can you do, people are what they are.'

I got out of the taxi and stood for a moment in the doorway of my building, looking out toward the street. The fog had lifted, and I had a clear view across the plaza for the first time in days; there were the empty hammocks and motionless trees, poised for the lashing that was on its way. This was the shapeless border between two times, where the best of each temporarily converged. I used to feel guilty for enjoying it. Fog was the counterpart to the red wind and, according to Max, I never wanted to pay the price for anything. Maybe he was right. Maybe that's why I spend my days riding the carousel of memory, sunk comfortably into the worn sofa of the past. Without the fog, the trees suddenly filled with details. Each branch followed its own capricious path; the leaves were no longer an amorphous mass of dull colors, you could see where one ended and the next began. I didn't feel guilty anymore for stopping to take in the streets the way they'd once been, during those brief moments when things were suddenly concrete, even if it meant that the wind was coming. I'd always thought a mystery was something hidden we could sense but never hold; now I know better. There is nothing more mysterious than the surface of things. The wind would be here any minute now, but I stretched the moment a bit longer, tempting fate until a patrol van turned the corner of the plaza and flashed its lights to force me inside.

During a red wind, armored police vans patrolled the city. Their job was to save the fearless from themselves and to keep people from jumping into the water. The guiding principle was ultimately decorum: they were there to keep a few exhibitionists from flaying themselves in public. The patrol van didn't stop, but it did slow down, trying to gauge my intentions. I made a placating gesture. Everything was fine.

The Health Minister was forced to resign after the incident with the fish. Then came a wave of scandals that would lead to the creation of a richer and more powerful Ministry, a kind of parallel state. The river didn't empty entirely, but no biologist or environmental expert could explain why some species were able to adapt. The new Ministry took charge of the situation, of the river with its mutant fish and the tannin-hued algae that was destroying the ecosystem. It began restructuring Clinics, closed the hillside factory where don Omar had worked all his life on the grounds that it was obsolete and unsanitary, and announced the construction of a new one.

I settled onto the couch as the trees swayed outside. There was a news report on television about the new national food-processing plant that had replaced the old factory. The aerial camera couldn't capture the whole complex, an oval-shaped structure that looked like a soccer stadium. They talked about it like a sporting event, too. They said: *triumph, historic, hope.* A transformative space—animals entered alive and left multiplied. The images showed huge stainless-steel vats, conveyor belts, robotic arms, and even a private laboratory. The very highest health standards for food and workers alike. They said: *regular inspections, surgical steel.* They said: *revolutionary system, pride of the nation.* My apartment was strange without Mauro in it. In a way, I wanted him to come back and fill the void, to bind me to my mechanisms of distraction. It wouldn't be long now: one more night spent listening to the wind howl in total darkness except for the shifting light of the television screen. By that time the next day, Mauro would be bursting into tears, and I would end up leaving the light on his bedside table lit for him. By then, I would be washing dishes, folding clothes, picking up toys.

On television, a man wearing a surgical cap and latex gloves with his suit and tie was explaining the safety standards at the new processing plant, and how its powerful, fast-moving machines utilized every last bit of the animal. He spoke with the enthusiasm of a camp counselor, as if he were injecting protein into the withered muscles of children with each word. Of course, the cameras were careful not to show the enormous swirls of meat toothpaste. I saw that stuff for the first time at the old factory, when Delfa would take me with her to drop off don Omar's lunch. It seemed light, airy: a piece of strawberry gum with all the flavor chewed out. Delfa and I would sit across from don Omar in a break room with aquamarine walls and watch him eat, his coveralls open in the front. We kept him company as he slurped his lentil broth and soaked his bread in what was left before snapping the container shut with a *clack clack* and handing it back to Delfa. Sometimes he'd show me around the factory; I can still remember the rancid stench of jellied meat and moldy dirt. They called it pink slime, and it smelled like congealed blood and the liquid Delfa used for cleaning the bathroom. Delfa smelled like that, too, on her fingers, which scrubbed don Omar's coveralls with antibacterial soap, removed his fabric shoelaces and soaked them in bleach before hanging them on the roof to dry.

Pink slime had a technical name, of course. Everything inconvenient has a technical name—insipid, colorless, odorless. But I liked calling it that. It reminded me of the pink river dolphins in the Amazon. My teacher told us they were born gray and turned pink over time. I repeated this once to Delfa, and I remember her saying something I couldn't understand at the time: Look at that, just the opposite of us.

'A safe, complete, nutritious meal,' said the man on television.

One more form of optimization. A machine heated the carcasses to extreme temperatures and spun them in a centrifuge until the last bits of lean meat separated from the animal's dirtier parts. Waste not, want not. When I was a little girl, Delfa would make me kiss the bread we were throwing out, no matter how stale it was, because God punished those who threw bread away without kissing it. Lemon and orange peels could also be used to flavor yerba mate. She would say: Think of all those children who have nothing. But instead I would think: Isn't that what don Omar's factory is for? He'd never let a child starve to death. Sometimes I thought don Omar owned the place. (He had a key, and when he showed me around, all the workers waved at me.) Why didn't he make more food? All he needed to do was push a button and a zillion little tubes of sausage would pop out. Because I already knew back then what pink slime was for: to multiply the meat and feed us, to create artificial ham and the quick-cooking hot dogs my mother liked. One minute in boiling water and all done. Delfa didn't want me eating that stuff, even though she and don Omar ate it all the time. Whenever we'd go to the supermarket she'd point to the poured hams, homogeneously pink and perfectly square. You see that? she'd ask. What part of the pig do you think that comes from? Have you ever seen a square hog? And when my mother asked her to buy frankfurters, Delfa would say: There's nothing like a real steak, señora Leonor. God will reward you for what you invest in your daughter.

Off camera, inside the steel vats, the centrifuged meat—a combination of tripe and scraps left over from the good cuts—would move on to the disinfection unit. The man in the tie pointed at the hoses that would spray the meat with ammonia. He said: *safety*. He said: *bioengineering*. He said: *superbacteria*. The ammonia killed the bacteria and helped bind the dregs that instinctively refused to agglutinate. Don Omar had explained this to me, too, while the three of us sat in that aquamarine room and he made little stacks of cheese and quince paste and drank his milky coffee with loads of sugar whipped into it by Delfa's quick, solid hands. I always watched her do it, *tsst, tsst, tsst*, all power and speed with the foam swelling to the sound of bubbles. We would talk about all kinds of things in that room until don Omar had to go back to work. Tell me something you learned in school recently, kid, he'd say. And I'd tell him about the pacu, the only fish with human teeth. A fish that could smile with whiter, straighter teeth than my own. How much would it hurt if one bit you? Or else I would say: Sharks have a whole bunch of teeth, in rows. How many rows? don Omar would ask. Ten, I'd say, making it up. Delfa would shake her head: We won't need teeth if no one's going to eat real meat anymore.

The camera soared into the air again. The roof of each division— beef, pork, poultry, legumes—was a different color, and from above they looked a lot like Mauro's Legos. The drone spun, giving us a 360-degree panorama. The fog, which looked like a stationary mass from below, seemed to move quickly up there, like downy strips of cloud. The camera wasn't flying very high, not even to the first ring; only army helicopters managed to cross the second. What would this new map look like from the sky? The lights that once crowded the coastline all gone dark, creating a new, unimaginable geography: the river without the red twinkle of fishing boats, the impenetrable sky without airplanes or stars.

Max and I are swimming in a river. The water is muddy and reaches our waists. He dives under and all I can see of him is the dark shadow of his undulating body. Then he bites me. I scream at almost the exact moment he emerges, gasping, from the water.

'What is it?' he asks.

'You bit me!'

He laughs and I think how I've always liked his smile, the way the left corner of his mouth pulls a bit higher than the right. He says he didn't bite me; he seems confused.

'You did. Right here on my leg,' I say.

I try to lift it and take a look at the wound, but my other foot slips on the muddy riverbed and I fall backward.

'Are you nuts? Why would I bite you?'

By now I'm angry and wade back to the shore. He follows me, defends himself.

'It must have been a pacu.'

We're sitting in the sand and looking at the red marks left by human teeth on the white skin of my leg.

'A pacu?' I repeat, but I'm thinking something else: that he'd always wanted to bite me, that he was always trying to devour me, one way or another.

Max examines the wound.

'At least it's not bleeding,' he says.

I want to bring up things he did in the past, but I hold back. It's different now; years have gone by and I need to learn how to trust. I can't ask him to open his mouth and prove that his bite doesn't match the marks left by the supposed pacu. We sit in silence. It was a pacu, I think. It was a pacu, I tell myself again as I let him rub my wound, as I let him knead it into something else.

Ever since I was a little girl I've had a strange kind of dream. Lucid dreams, they're called: you know you're dreaming but you can't wake up. When I opened my eyes, the show had ended and all that was on was the black-and-white static that runs when there's nothing left to air. I didn't have the energy to go to bed. The hat I'd made for Mauro's birthday a few weeks earlier sat on top of the television— a hand-painted cardboard cone that was beginning to come unstuck. I'd needed to flip a hamburger carton inside out because I couldn't find any arts and crafts supplies at Valdivia's store. I ran my tongue along my gums; they were painful and swollen. A little pressure and they'd release the acidic taste of blood. Something inside me wanted to go into free fall, to sink into a heap of trash as vast and deep as the river. I needed to resist the pull of the elastic, the feeling that I could have done something to keep the red wind from reaching him. I thought about Max, all six feet of him crammed into that hospital bed. I thought about the truck that had come for his things—just a few suitcases and boxes because he'd never helped pay for any of the furniture—while I watched the movers from the balcony. The children shouting in the schoolyard. My mother saying: You cut out a cancer. But I don't know what came first. Memories, too, are recyclable waste.

Who said that?

She did.

And what else?

Nothing.

No gestures? No change in her expression?

I forget.

You're forgetting the most important part.

Words aren't enough for you?

Body language confirms or negates any message.

What if I tell you she frowned?

You're lying.

I am.

No one says what they mean: it's the face that speaks.

Mauro will be back at noon. I will be waiting for him at the window looking out at the sky, which will be orange like a hot iron with a few thin clouds that won't gather fully before the next wind. I'll watch the SUV drive around the plaza and into the garage of my building. The apartment will be ready for Mauro. I'll open the door and wait for them in the hall. I'll hear their footsteps on the stairs, followed by silence as they walk along the carpeted halls. When they reach the third floor, I'll be able to make out Mauro's labored breathing.

This time he will come alone with the driver, who will be carrying two boxes of food. The driver's head will be hidden behind the boxes, but I'll hear him puff and strain to keep his balance, his back slightly arched. Mauro will be pouting. He will refuse to kiss me hello and will head inside without saying a word. The driver, sweaty and flushed, will set the two boxes on the floor. Mauro's Spider-Man backpack will be hanging from his shoulder. He will hand it to me, along with an envelope containing that month's pay.

'I guess time really is money,' I'll say.

The driver will remain serious, professional, as if he and I weren't the same species: two lackeys at the service of the currency in that envelope.

'The elevator's broken?'

'They don't repair it anymore. Anyway, the exercise does us good. Was it a long drive?'

'The highway's tricky these days. Checkpoints, inspections. They're looking for contraband.'

Just then, like a sinister detail, the alarm will sound. I'll see a flash of panic in the driver's eyes and will then watch his body force itself to stay calm.

'Wouldn't you rather wait inside?'

He will shrug me off.

'The car is reinforced.'

Then he will stare at the envelope in my hand.

'You're not going to count it?'

He probably wants to know how much it costs for someone to take responsibility for a child who can't tell the difference between a finger and a sausage. I wasn't the only one who had tried to care for Mauro, but I was the only one who'd lasted more than a few months.

'Don't worry,' I'll say. 'I'm sure it's fine.' We'll have to raise our voices over the alarm. 'See you next month.'

'Sure,' he'll say without much conviction as he retreats toward the stairs.

I'd seen the driver two or three times before that day. It was usually Mauro's mother who brought him, though every so often he'd come with his father—a simple, quiet man nothing at all like his wife, who, if she were a house, would be full of secret corners and hidden doors. I stood in the hallway a bit longer, even though the sound of the driver's footsteps was being drowned out. Mauro was frightened; each time he arrived he seemed to have forgotten this life riddled with safety protocols, sealed windows, air filters, water that had to be boiled twice before drinking, the alarm that interrupted our daily life.

When I stepped inside the apartment, Mauro was sitting on the rug in front of the television with his head tilted to the side, covering one ear.

'It's almost over,' I said. 'Do you want to tell me about riding horses?'

He gestured no by rubbing his head slightly against his shoulder.

'Do you want to sing the song about the groggy froggy?'

Also no.

He opened his backpack and rummaged around inside. He couldn't find what he was looking for, so he dumped everything onto the floor and grabbed a book from the pile.

'What's that? A new book? About dinosaurs?'

'Tyrannousauce,' he said, holding it out to me.

We sat on the sofa to leaf through it. Outside, the wind was picking up dust and grime. Papers and scraps of garbage flew through the air. The pinkish clouds had vanished and the sky was that intense hue it took on, like raw meat dripping its juices over us. Mauro stared intently at the drawings of dinosaurs, but he was holding his left hand up to his ear; his other hand rested on my arm. His body language did not match his size. He looked like he'd been inflated, like a tire that couldn't take even a tiny bit more air, with his chubby cheeks, one eye that was always half-shut, and his mouth, which was small but not too small to devour whatever came near it without even so much as chewing. A little piranha mouth, quick and unrelenting. Even so, I felt like I knew Mauro; I believed I could anticipate the things that would make him nervous, that would make him shrink into himself like a mollusk, sheltered inside a body that was pure instinct. Maybe this was why he had a calming effect on me. With him, I didn't feel like I needed to hide any part of myself. Mauro was a safe space where I could lower my guard. It had always been the opposite with Max, even now as he lay in a hospital bed, having finally become a demigod profaned each day with needles and sensors in the name of science. The doctors knew all his numbers, the data of his unique chemistry. They'd observed his skin under a microscope—the precise mosaic of his cells, the movement of their death. And even so, they didn't know him.

'*Tarbosaurus*,' I read, 'the alarming lizard.'

Mauro pointed to a drawing underneath letters drawn in dripping red: *Carnivorous Dinosaurs*.

'And this one?'

'*Tyrannosaurus rex*.'

'And this one?'

'*Dilophosaurus*, the two-crested lizard.'

His finger, its short nail sticky and red with remnants of cotton candy or a strawberry lollipop, slid along the page.

'*Spinosaurus aegyptiacus*,' I said.

'And this one?'

'Shark-toothed lizard, *Carcharo . . . dontosaurus*.'

What had been going through Max's mind? The alarm had sounded, a wind was clearly coming, but he'd gone out to the garden anyway. It was November, six months after he'd moved out.

Things would have been different if I had been there, which was maybe why he did it: to explore the limits of his new freedom. Like I said, it was November, and the epidemic showed no signs of letting up. Cold and wind and despair. They hadn't ordered the evacuation of the coast yet, but the Ministry had just established the quarantine wing at Clinics. We were always on alert. That day, Max went out to gather firewood even though the fog had lifted and sand was beginning to prick at his calves. Arrogance, or self-sacrifice? He walked slowly across the yard, gathering pine cones and the few sticks untouched by the humidity that softened the earth and covered everything with fungus. Two weeks later, his legs began to itch and red blotches appeared on his arms.

'And this one?' asked Mauro.

'*Giganotosaurus*,' I read. 'The giant lizard of the south.'

'Giant,' he repeated. 'Does he eat?'

'Yes. And what else do dinosaurs do?'

'Eat.'

While Mauro played, I took the money from the envelope, counted it, and stuck it in the safe with the rest. Everything valuable was in that safe: currency decorated with near-extinct local fauna that offered the illusion of buying a future; containers of emergency food—gherkins, pickled onions, peaches in syrup, canned corn. I kept the key hidden above the bathroom mirror, part of a whole collection in different sizes and weights that I could recognize by touch. Each one opened a different padlock: refrigerator, kitchen cabinets, the drawers in my room. When it came to Mauro's hunger, you could never be too careful. Once, his mother told me, they'd needed to pump his stomach. He'd eaten the entire contents of the medicine cabinet, which they kept locked ever since. You need eyes in the back of your head, the woman had said, you always need to be on your toes. She looked tired, and I thought I detected a trace of pain in her voice. But maybe not; maybe she was just telling me how to do my job.

So what if I leave?

So what if you leave?

Is that an answer or another one of your koans?

Are you asking my permission?

No.

What, then?

I saw you the other day.

Where?

In a dream.

Mauro had come back in a terrible mood and refused to follow the rules I tried to teach him. They paid me for that, too: to teach him the same thing over and over, the same no-nos, the same routines, only to have his mother destroy our progress every month. They paid me not to complain, to keep him on a short leash, and to invent songs that distracted him from his hunger. He'd come back from the countryside with all his clothes filthy: dirt and grass stains on his pants, food dribbled down his shirts. I scrubbed until my hands turned red, which made me think of Delfa. I had dreamed about her the night before. Delfa would have known how to brighten those whites, how to remove those difficult stains. She would have a home remedy for each one: baking soda or vinegar or lemon, maybe.

In my dream, Delfa was wearing the same apron and shoes as always. Nothing about her had changed, but she was like a stranger to me. I (not me as a girl, but the woman I am today) looked at her suspiciously. Delfa shouted at a dog that wouldn't stop barking; she was furious because the dog had been following her and hadn't let her sleep for days. Suddenly she turned and looked at me. If a body puts the sleep from a dog's eyes in his own, she said, either the Devil or all the angels of heaven will appear before him. The dog kept barking, but didn't seem like it meant to bite. I grabbed the scruff of its neck with one hand, and with the other I wiped the sticky substance from its rabid eyes. Then I woke up.

I can't remember if Delfa had her wig yet in the dream. One day she showed up at our house with a wiry wig that was supposed to be blond but looked like it had been coated with ash. The wig shifted on her head and I'd watch her adjust it in the mirror, attaching it with countless black bobby pins. The treatment had opened cracks in her fingers that bled and burned when she bathed me or chopped onions. I remember her standing in the kitchen making me rice cro-quetas; I remember the hairs she would leave on the sofa cushions and later the synthetic wig that was never flecked with dandruff.

'I want a wig, too,' I said once as Delfa was doing my braids. I liked to sit on her lap as she ran a soft brush through my hair. Her touch made me sleepy, the way she slowly dragged the brush downward, even long after my hair was silky and free of tangles. Now I think Delfa's hands were another certainty, just like the summers in San Felipe, and there was nothing I craved more than that predictability.

'Is that so? And why do you want a wig?'

'So I never have to wash my hair.'

Delfa laughed. She always got soap in my eyes when she washed my hair, and my baths had become a nightmare. My mother thought it was *sinister*, the way Delfa left hairs around the house. She'd get home from work and flop down on the living room sofa, always exhausted, her legs spread and her blouse unbuttoned. She would take off her earrings and her rings and put them on the side table. She'd ask me to turn on the television, to change the channel, to turn up the volume or adjust the antenna, and if she found a blond hair on the cushions or on the arm of the sofa she would pick it up between two fingers as if it were a worm, and say: How sinister. This was shortly after I began calling Delfa 'Mom.' I did it behind my mother's back, without a hint of childhood innocence. I knew it was the greatest possible betrayal.

I'd made two drawings for Mother's Day. Both featured birds, trees, fruit, a house, and two stick figures, one tall and one little. One drawing said *Leonor* in glitter glue, and the other said *Delfa*. A few years ago, when I finally managed to track down don Omar and went to visit him, he told me that Delfa always carried the drawing with her, folded up in her wallet. He'd found it going through her things for the funeral.

'She shows up in my dreams, sometimes,' I told him.

'What does she say?'

'Nothing.'

The drawing still existed. Don Omar handed it to me as if he'd been waiting a long time for that moment. I opened it: the paper was translucent, about to crumble at the folds. The glitter had come unstuck in places and all that was left of Delfa's name were a few letters and the grayish trace of others.

'We never needed to talk much,' said don Omar. 'The less you talk, kid, the closer you are.'

Max and I did nothing but talk. It was our substitute for physical contact. I never felt desire as a girl or teenager; if I thought about my body at all, it was as currency. I knew, more by intuition than experience, that I could get certain things with it. I didn't see this as negative, but it wasn't anything to celebrate, either. So when Max started withdrawing, absorbed by his search for himself, I adjusted easily to the situation. I believed our relationship existed on another plane and, deep down, it made me proud. We would spend the whole night talking and then, as birds announced the dawn and we lay exhausted from digging around inside ourselves with words, I would let his body agonize on top of mine, inside of mine, until we fell asleep. You suffer from overcivilization, Max would say, but then he'd wrap his arms around me, stick his tongue in my mouth, and we'd both laugh. What purpose does that tongue of yours serve anyway? He used to say he had a dual-channel tongue, that mine was mono. Over the years, those things that had once seemed charming became the barbs we'd hurl at one another.

One of the last times we slept together, Max wrapped his arms around me from behind and slid his hands inside my shirt. We'd already turned out the light, and I had spent that whole Saturday with Mauro. My body went tense. I pretended to sleep while he tugged off my pants and underwear. Then I felt his fingers drive into me; he moved them like someone looking desperately for something, getting angrier by the moment. I didn't make a sound, either of pleasure or objection, when he rolled me onto my back. I was dry and he struggled to penetrate me. I felt my flesh resist and heard the noise, or maybe it was just the sensation, of plastic stretching, like when someone puts on a new rubber glove. Max asked me to move a little for him and I said: I'm tired. I can see that, he said, pulling out. He flopped onto his back, exaggerating the gesture to shake the wooden bed frame. That's not what I meant, I said. I could feel his body, long and eternal, to my left, but not a bit of our skin was touching. Go to sleep, he said. What I had meant was that I was tired deep in my bones, so deep I couldn't find the strength to do anything for him, for us, or even for myself.

I couldn't talk much with Mauro, which changed the equation. I felt clumsy, neutralized. In the beginning, when I first met him, I couldn't separate him from his illness. His condition—being a sick child—defined him and denied him the right to be anything else. I hadn't yet quit my job at the agency and was taking care of Mauro on the weekends in order to spend as little time as possible with Max. We still lived together, but our relationship was just a pit of resentment. He felt trapped; I felt betrayed. Our life was built around honoring the kids we'd once been, even though we had almost nothing in common with them anymore.

During one of those weekends, I decided to take Mauro to a restaurant. A little girl at the table next to ours couldn't take her eyes off him. Mauro usually ate so fast he could barely taste his food, but that wasn't why the girl was staring; she couldn't have been more than three years old and something had caught her attention about the way he played with his napkin, folding it as many times as he could. I had told him that no piece of paper, no matter how big, could be folded in half more than seven times and he was testing it out. Next to her, the girl's older brother chewed absentmindedly while playing a video game. His shoulders were hunched forward, like he wanted to crawl into the device. Their mother, arms crossed and food untouched, drilled into him with an indignant glare, but the boy didn't even notice. The woman sighed loudly and turned to see what had caught the girl's attention. That was when she saw Mauro. She studied his adipose arms, the jowls disfiguring his neck, and his small, puffy, strangely nimble hands.

'Sebastian, put that thing down,' she snapped. She spoke so forcefully that the boy looked up. He shrugged.

'I lost, anyway,' he said, resting the game beside his plate.

But the woman's eyes were still on Mauro. Her expression had softened: relief, maybe. Or maybe superiority. Her children might not be perfect, but theirs were normal problems, minor headaches. Just a matter of setting boundaries, of being firm but gentle so no one could accuse her of being a bad mother. Such a difficult balance to strike: motherhood was a real minefield, any false step might blow you to pieces. But then she'd see a case like Mauro, poor thing, and that would put it all in perspective. The woman went on studying him, fear tugging at the corners of her mouth. Just as I was about to say something, the little girl squeezed the ketchup too hard, and a thick spurt buried the fries on her plate.

'What are you doing?' the woman asked. She was angry again. The girl's fingers were smeared with red, and she held them up as if saying hello. 'What, Micaela? You're going to eat all that? Do you want to end up'—here, she lowered her voice and leaned over so her face was level with the girl's—'like that little boy?'

At that, I did stand up. The woman must have noticed, because she froze, gripping one of her daughter's dirty little hands. I was about to say *that little boy* is sick when I realized: I needed to justify him, I needed to turn Mauro into a syndrome to ease a total stranger's discomfort—and my own, I guess. Mauro would never be able to escape it. I could; I could walk away, forget the whole thing, reduce it to an anecdote. He would always be the vessel of that illness.

As time went by, I began to think of the syndrome as an impostor that had taken over Mauro's body. It wasn't even a gene that determined his hunger, but the absence of one: a bit of information missing from chromosome fifteen—in quiniela, the niña bonita. At first, he'd seemed like any other baby except for his weak sucking reflex, lack of muscle, and difficulty holding his head up. An insatiable monster-to-be. What is it like to feel constant hunger? A hunger that drowns out every other thought. The need to quiet that voice, to fill that inconceivable void. Until he turned three, Mauro had been the apple of his mother's eye: a happy, chubby boy—not the sharpest tack, but never a picky eater; he didn't even mind broccoli, olives, or polenta. But something happened one day. She walked into the kitchen and found him with a chicken she'd just taken out of the freezer. He was gnawing on the grainy white plaster of its frost-flecked skin and didn't even notice her standing there.

'He doesn't think about me, or you,' she will say to me one day that still seems distant. 'He only thinks about his next meal.'

It takes a massive ego to name an incurable disease after yourself. The illness didn't belong to anyone who never felt a cavernous hunger in their own stomach, an implacable urge to chew on walls or swallow trash. That day, we left the restaurant and walked three blocks down to the rambla. It was a Saturday and the whole city had rushed out to enjoy the sun—not for any reason we know today, which no one could have anticipated, but simply because it was early May and every warm afternoon seemed like some kind of miscalculation. People were out jogging or skateboarding in clothes unsuited to the season, as if this error of nature were a bubble they could inhabit. Mauro sat down on a cement bench, facing the river. He probably wasn't feeling great, his stomach struggling to contain all that food, but he didn't let on.

A cruise ship was heading into port and there were cargo vessels on the horizon. Mauro counted them. We made a game of it. It was a normal day, not the beginning of anything. A few months later, the algae would spread across the river and turn its surface a deep burgundy. A beautiful phenomenon; we went down to the rambla to see it. It didn't seem dangerous. The river used to be brown or green, depending on an optical illusion produced by the sky; now, entire sections of it looked red—sometimes in a long strip extending along the horizon, sometimes a crimson circle like a fiery tongue emerging from the water. Our river was suddenly a patchwork quilt, a light show. The children clapped and the adults took pictures; Mauro seemed hypnotized by the flaming sea. But the euphoria didn't last. After a few weeks, we awoke to a shoreline carpeted with dead fish. That was when the Ministry sent divers to inspect the riverbed.

And what will you look for there?

The same thing as you.

You're angry that the past you love so much doesn't matter to me anymore.

You're saying you wouldn't go back?

Why would I?

I go back, sometimes.

In your mind, you mean?

Something like that.

The mind is a dangerous place.

The phone rang at seven in the morning. I knew it was my mother even before I picked up. I'd asked her a million times not to call so early, but it was typical of her not to register anything that was asked of her. I got up, unsteady on my feet, afraid the ringing would wake Mauro. He'd fallen asleep around midnight, after another crying fit. He'd refused to close his eyes and didn't want me to turn out the light. He kicked the blankets to the floor and made a tent of his sheet. I had sat beside him on the edge of his bed, trying to calm him while he talked to himself. They weren't even recognizable words; he'd withdrawn into his invented language, with its long, keening vowels. His communication seemed to regress each time he came back from the country. I suspected that no one there spoke to him, that they let him run loose outside like a little animal, sticking his fingers into every bug-filled hole he saw. But I was probably exaggerating. Someone must have been watching him, some other nanny who didn't have the energy to scold him for every bite he shoved into his mouth, or to talk with him much.

I got to the telephone before the third ring. The living room was cold, and dawn announced its arrival with a feeble light.

'How is he?'

'Unmanageable.'

'You know what I think about all this.'

Three black slats, two white lines. I'd forgotten to close the blinds the night before and light framed the wooden strips in the upper third of the window: the slats a deep black, white lines interrupting their darkness with a dirty glow.

'It isn't worth it, dear.'

'Mom, it's seven in the morning.'

'I know what time it is.'

The light hurt my eyes. Three, two, three. If I closed one eye and then the other, if I alternated them, the strips seemed to move. Up and down. Three two, three two. Just a millimeter. The glow left a bright trail inside my eyelids.

'Do *you* know what time it is?' she asked. 'I'll tell you: it's time for you to do something.'

Threetwo: inhale. Threetwo: exhale. No shadows fell across the parquet floor, just the black hollows of a few missing pieces of wood. The geometric pattern extended in a zigzag, like arrows, keeping the eye in motion.

'It won't be long now,' I said, in a remarkable feat of self-control. 'You'll see.'

'That's what I told your cousin Cecilia when we spoke yesterday. Do you know what the inlanders think of us?'

'That we're crazy?'

'Worse. That we're a lost cause.'

'Tell her we'll send her a postcard from Brazil.'

'Brazil . . . right. And what do you propose we do there?'

'I don't know, live?'

'You're talking as if you were dead.'

Two. Two. Two.

'Am I?'

Three.

'You're depressed, dear. You're making yourself sick. And for what? How long do you plan to go on like this?'

'I assume you're talking about Max again.'

'Who else would I be talking about? What do you think he's doing right now? I'll tell you what: he's living his life. And just look at you.'

Day is breaking, or trying to: the light presses against the blinds, pushing through the lines and darkening the slats. Twothree, twothree. A faint shadow forms on the parquet, the straight line of the bottom slat. But the sun will lose this battle, just like I will. My breath quickens.

'It won't be long, Mom, I almost have enough saved up.'

'All day locked inside with that little boy.'

'Do you want to go with me or not? I'm not forcing you.'

'Go where?'

'Brazil, where else? What are we talking about?'

'I don't know what you're talking about. I'm talking about your life. Look at yourself.'

It wasn't so much a noise as a different kind of silence that made me turn around. With my back to the window, I saw Mauro standing in the half-light, rubbing his eyes. His pajamas were tight under his arms and around his belly, his legs, too; some of the seams were beginning to give out.

'Look what we did,' I said, 'we woke Mauro up.' But she ignored me.

'Do you have any idea what it's like for a mother to see her daughter like this?' I had stopped counting my breaths and could only feel the rage throbbing in my throat. Behind me, the white lines sank their spikes into my back. 'I don't know why I call, when all it does is upset me.'

'Maybe we shouldn't talk, then.'

'Right,' she said. 'Maybe we shouldn't.'

'Right.'

'Right.'

And she hung up.

It had been ten days since Mauro's return and the alarm still sounded daily. It was a phenomenon—another phenomenon—called El Príncipe. Now I can say all that was a beginning, but at the time it seemed like an end. I thought that what was ending was my relationship with Max. The problem is that beginnings and endings overlap, so you think something is ending when in reality something else is getting its start. It's like staring at clouds: they change shape as they move, but if you keep your eyes on them they seem pretty consistent. That fluffy rabbit is still a rabbit—maybe it's a little wider, or it has shorter ears and a blurry muzzle; maybe it's breaking up a bit and has lost its tail or a bit of fur, but you can still see it. On the other hand, if you glance away for just a second and then look back, you won't find any trace of the former rabbit, just a mass of clouds.

Now, for example: am I in a beginning or an end? It's like a long pause, time suspended.

I hadn't been able to calm Mauro down. He still got out of bed at night and rummaged through everything; he'd even broken a shampoo bottle, his anxiety was out of control. I had warned his mother that it was getting harder and harder for him to make the transition, to adapt to our confinement. Even with the filters, the air in the apartment was unbreathable after so many days with the windows closed. The news only ran stories about the misery El Príncipe brought with it. Forty infections in one week; twice as many as in recent months. The red wind could penetrate the smallest crevice and some people woke up to find themselves in a prickling, acidic cyclone. Four or five days later, their skin would begin to peel off. Before that, the symptoms were like the flu: cough, fatigue, general malaise. That was all we knew, aside from the rumors. There was nothing on television about muscles left exposed to the air, about children and the elderly flayed by the fabric of their shirts. *If you develop any of these symptoms, go immediately to Clinics.* The message ran along the bottom of the screen. *Keep your face mask with you at all times.* On a loop, like those conveyor belts at the airport. *This is a message from the Ministry of Health. Every life is unique.*

Mauro's mother had asked me to call the doctor in case of emergency, said that they would pick him up and have him admitted to a state-of-the-art clinic. The best, she said, *state of the art*, and I think it embarrassed her a little. Then she handed me a stack of money. Her hand was soft, but it was the imposed softness of imported creams and nightly skin care regimens. Mauro had been like this for ten days and I hadn't called the state-of-the-art clinic. I was afraid of what they might do to him if they saw him so nervous and aggressive. Who wouldn't have been nervous? The alarm sounded nonstop, and the wind rattled the windows. They'd never said it straight-out, but Mauro's parents also paid me to keep doctors, injections, sedatives, and restraints far away from him.

On television they were announcing that the contamination had spread, but they didn't say where. *Help us avoid overcrowding! Don't go to Clinics unless you feel sick.* The message from the Ministry kept cycling through like an infinite loop, and eventually you just forgot it was there. *Help us keep you safe. Every life is unique.* How much was left of my escape route? The algae was closing in on me, and I didn't even know what units I could use to measure that distance. Months? Red winds? Visits to Max?

I'd called my mother every day since our last conversation and had gotten no answer. Maybe she was sick, or maybe the wind had caught up with her and she was lying motionless on the sofa, shadows anticipating the hollows of her empty sockets. Or maybe she was doing it on purpose, ignoring the phone to give me what I *deserved*. Another word she loved. We all deserved something, good or bad, and apparently she was in charge of deciding what. My cousin Cecilia deserved the life she had. The schoolteacher deserved a good man. The politicians deserved only the *worst*. (But what was that? Death? Suffering? A stay at Clinics?) I know what she wanted: she wanted me to drop everything—my job, my dreams, and even my sanity—and run to her, terrified and trembling, having finally understood the importance of her existence. That way, she could feel like things were back to how they should be. But I wasn't going to do that. No. I wasn't going to drop my end of the rope. This was our familiar tug-of-war: I pulled, she pulled more, and for as long as we canceled each other out it seemed like neither would ever take another step, not in her direction or in mine. A possible circle of Hell, this eternal skirmish with my mother. The tug-of-war nearly always ended the same way: muscles stiff and hands rubbed raw, I'd eventually give in. Then she would loosen her grip and, ever the benevolent victor, offer me a small gesture or kind word. The performance of affection. But it wasn't going to work this time. I couldn't leave Mauro alone; he'd suck the whitewash from the walls, eat the lint that collected around the base of the couch. Why did I care so much? When had lint ever killed anyone? Why couldn't I tell my mother the truth about Max? Would she take pity on him now that he was sick? No. She would just say that he finally got what he deserved. And what did I deserve? My mother was careful never to be too explicit; now and then she just said that I deserved *something else*. She didn't need to be judge and jury with me—I enforced my own punishments.

Ha ha ha.

No one laughs like that.

Hee hee hee.

Are you laughing at me?

Yes.

At my face?

Yes.

I don't deserve that.

Do you remember that saint who fell in love with a dolphin?

A gray dolphin or a pink one?

What difference does that make?

Hee hee hee.

It wasn't unusual for us to wake up without power. The blackouts had been getting worse for months. The fluctuations in voltage threatened to short out the appliances, so as soon as the lights started to flicker it was best to unplug everything, even the refrigerator, which after a while would let out a noxious stream of water as the meat thawed. Again.

'Light no?' asked Mauro, pushing the remote control buttons.

'No,' I replied. 'Again.'

Mauro had drawn a picture of dinosaurs eating pizza. At least, that's what he said it was when I asked, because the drawing itself was a bunch of colorful lines through a big yellow circle. All his games and conversations revolved around food; hoping for anything else would be like asking him not to breathe. The strange thing was his obsession with pizza. Maybe that's what they gave him in the countryside, when his parents took him. With me he mostly ate a meat pâté that came in little cups like yogurt and reminded me of astronaut food. It was called Meatrite, and it was made to go a long way, either spread on or stuffed into various things. Nearly all our meals smelled like it, and sometimes I thought its odor had permeated the whole apartment, even my skin.

Mauro walked over and dropped his drawing in my lap.

'Is this for me?' I asked. He didn't answer; he'd already sat back down to work on more pictures. He drew angrily, grabbing the pencil wrong and catching it on the seams in the parquet floor, where it would leave a hole in the paper.

The worst thing about those days when the power went out wasn't my fear that the frozen food would spoil. It was the boredom of being alone with Mauro, without the sound of the television to daze and protect me. I cooked, cleaned up all the food scraps, kept our provisions under lock and key, and took out the garbage every night, tossing it in with the rotting bags on the corner by the plaza; if there was a wind, I simply brought the bag down to the building's lobby and piled it on the stench that got worse by the day. Mauro and I did exercises inside the apartment; we went up and down the stairs. I'd taught him to jump elastics, which we stretched between the legs of two chairs, and hopscotch. They paid me for every calorie he burned and every gram of fat that melted off his body. They paid me to keep him moving, to make him pant and puff as he climbed the stairs all the way up to the eighth floor. To invent hula-hoop championships and let him win. I'd lost weight, too. By the end of each day I was so exhausted that I fell asleep before my head even hit the pillow. They paid me for that, too. For turning my body over to Mauro. Or was it to the syndrome? They hadn't only bought my time, they'd also bought my energy; they'd bought my muscles, my sore quadriceps and shaking arms after playing airplane. I lived for the syndrome—I lived to wear out that insatiable animal and reach the real Mauro, even if just for a moment. The one behind the hunger. When the syndrome couldn't take any more, when it collapsed in defeat, reeking of sweat and of hands dragged around the entire building, that's when I knew I'd done my job.

Later that same morning we heard sounds in the hallway. We stuck our heads out the door, Mauro hiding behind my legs, and saw a medical transport team wheel a gurney up to apartment 503. All of them in German respirator masks. They said something to us; I couldn't understand what, but from their gestures I could tell we were supposed to go back inside and close the door. I pulled it mostly shut, but not all the way. Through the crack, I could see my neighbor from 503 come out in his underwear with his face bright red like he'd gotten a bad sunburn and white and purple blotches across his torso. They helped him onto the gurney, but as they were about to pull the sheet over him, he lifted his hand feebly as if to shield himself and said: No, please. They took him away like that, half-naked and red, about to lose his skin. We followed the rest of the operation from the window. The health transport team tried to maneuver the gurney into the van without the man falling off. I pressed my eyes shut so I could picture Max protected by a bubble of light. Sometimes I honestly believed it was me, my desire, keeping him alive. The vehicle pulled away and when Mauro asked me where they were taking our neighbor I told him to leave me alone.

'Go play in your room for a minute, okay?'

My gums were bleeding and I'd been pressing my tongue to them for a while, swallowing the metallic taste that ran between my teeth. The sound of Mauro's incomprehensible language reached me as a murmur from his room.

I listened to him playing for over an hour until a gagging sound caught my attention.

'Mauro?' I called, but the only answer was another *caahh, caahh*. When I got to him, his mouth was half-open and his eyes were watering. What is it, Mauro? He was trying to swallow something, but his throat rejected it with an asthmatic wheeze. He couldn't even cough. Mauro, what are you eating? The pale blue of his skin contrasted sharply with his lips and the rims of his eyes, which were purple, violent. I managed to pry open his mouth, stick two fingers down his throat, and remove a warm, wet cotton ball. The package, which I'd brought out the night before to clean a cut on his knee, sat on the nightstand and now Mauro was struggling to reach it. Leave that alone, I said, that's not for eating, while he coughed and gasped, catching his breath. Once the package was out of sight, he began to cry and sniffle.

'All right,' I said. 'It's over.'

Through his snot I heard him say he was hungry. To calm him down, I offered him a popsicle. Sitting on the parquet floor, he let the colored water dribble down his hands and wrists, then drip onto his legs from his elbows. I didn't scold him. He was circumspect, licking the ice pop furiously, analyzing which side was melting faster, trying to anticipate the drops that formed more quickly than his tongue could move. When it was all gone, he nibbled the soft, reddened stick a bit and then threw it against the wall.

'Go wash your hands.'

'No,' he retorted, suddenly glum.

He waved his hands in the air to dry them. I imagined their cold stickiness.

'Come here, then.'

He sat at my feet in front of the television, among his scattered toys, and started playing with his Legos. Lately, he'd been making dinosaurs. His favorite was a kind of alebrije with a yellow tail and a blue head. His shirt was moist with tears and his arm still bore the red marks of my fingers. He hadn't even felt them: his pain threshold was so high that once he'd stuck a fork into his arm like it was attached to someone else. The night before, he'd cut his knee and hadn't realized it; I was the one who'd seen the dried blood all over his leg. Another reason why it was so important to keep an eye on him, to protect him from himself.

I don't think I felt fear when he choked on that cotton ball. I was shaken, but not frightened. The feeling of doing terrible harm to someone other than myself. One minute more and he could have suffocated. Did I love him, then? I've always confused fear with love: that unstable ground, that landslide zone. Mauro was my charge, and little by little he was also becoming my responsibility.

His bulging abdomen moved under his shirt with each quick, shallow breath.

'Deep breaths,' I said, and mimed filling my lungs and holding the air in. He copied me, puffing his cheeks. Then he blew the air out as hard as he could. He found this very funny.

'Goofball,' I said.

When he laughed, his eyes disappeared into the flesh of his face and his little red tongue and milk teeth peeked out from between his lips.

'Sure. Very funny, goofball.'

He lifted the half-made *Giganotosaurus* to his mouth.

'No biting.'

Without a second's pause, he threw it as hard as he could and the southern lizard shattered into colorful rectangles in the corner. I stood casually and walked over to gather the pieces.

'Why, Mauro? Look at what you did to your poor dinosaur.'

As soon as I handed him the pieces he threw them again, this time under the sofa. He looked at me out of the corner of his eye, trying to gauge the limits of my patience.

'Sleeping,' he said.

'Don't make him sleep like that.'

'Why?'

'Because there's a mean dog under there and he might get bitten.'

Mauro managed to squat in front of the couch, his hair dangling stringy in front of his eyes. He squinted at the Lego pieces scattered in the darkness but couldn't muster the courage to reach for them.

Which sounds better: chaos or trampoline?

Chaos.

Human or struggle?

Human.

Crime or crumb?

Crumb.

Sober or somber?

Somber.

Furious or fleeting?

We all expected that the birds would meet the same fate as the fish, that one day they'd start falling from the sky like ripe fruit. We thought we'd watch them all suddenly crash to earth. But no. Instead, we stopped seeing birds. No one really noticed it happening because they left gradually, in flocks. Unlike the fish, the birds vanished without furious cawing or futile deaths. They simply vacated the sky. One morning the parks were silent and someone on television said they had migrated, and it was like we'd been given permission to notice it. People went crazy; they headed for the parks with their binoculars, they filled the plazas with breadcrumbs. No one ever saw another bird, not even a pigeon. They gathered a panel of experts on television. The show was called *Will the Birds Come Back?* and it was the most-watched program in history. They invited a State biologist, a civil servant, and several public figures—the usual cast of charlatans. There was a large seagull painted on the back wall of the set. They said: *migration, sightings, flyways*. They said: *GPS, radiotelemetry*. They talked and talked, but silence had claimed the sky. After that, I'd sometimes think I saw a sparrow on a tree branch, heard a caw or the flutter of wings. But no. The birds left us to face the red wind alone.

I wonder whether the dog that followed Delfa around in my dream might have something to do with the rabid dog we buried alive. We were at least fifteen or twenty kids who summered in San Felipe: the six children of my mother's lifelong friend, Albertito; Ximena and Maite, the acrobat twins; all the divers' children in the co-op apartments; and Max, two houses down from mine. We got our seaweed fritters from the only restaurant in town, where all the divers' wives worked, but if you knew José Luis's mother you could buy them right from her, and she'd pass them to you through the kitchen window in a little plastic basket. José Luis was the youngest diver and an only child. Sometimes he'd bring us fritters wrapped in paper napkins transparent with grease that shredded between our fingers. We also ate mussels fresh from the rocks, fried fish, and silversides that the men went out to the cliffs with kerosene lanterns to catch. During the day we filled the water tanks, and at night we lit lanterns, candles, or flashlights. Whenever we set foot in someone's house, each child had to pump water into the tank ten times and gather pine needles to make fires. That endless, infinite state of well-being was my idea of happiness. Danger adopted more visible, though sometimes also treacherous, forms: scorpions, thistles, jellyfish, giant waves.

The day that dog followed us, Max and I were with Albertito's eldest, Alejandro, who was two years older than us, José Luis, and the acrobat twins. We were on an expedition to the Elephant, the tallest, most dangerous rock on the point. A dog started barking at us on the way. Albertito's son, who always carried a stick with him, threatened the dog and it backed off but kept growling, baring the sharp teeth in its shiny red gums.

'He must see something,' said Max. 'They have different senses than we do.'

'Infrared vision,' said José Luis.

'That's dumb,' Albertito's son shut him up. 'They see with their noses.'

'Maybe there's a ghost,' said one of the twins, either Ximena or Maite, with tendrils of fear in her eyes.

'What if it's rabid?' I asked.

The dog was still with us as we got further out on the rocks. It had stopped barking, but it followed us from about a meter back, eyeing us suspiciously like it was waiting for something, like it knew we weren't allowed on the Elephant. A diver had fallen while trying to climb it to make his jump from there. He'd made a bet with his friends, but he fell backward and broke his neck, dying impaled on the rocks.

'It must have the diver's soul inside it,' said José Luis. He'd gone pale and was beginning to second-guess our excursion. 'Maybe he's trying to tell us something.'

That was how it started, with José Luis saying what he said, because fear is contagious and spreads from one person to the next like dominoes falling. The only way to stop it is to do something radical, disruptive, but we didn't know that yet. At least, not in words.

'He's guarding the rock,' said Max. 'The ghost won't let us climb it.'

It didn't occur to any of us that the dog was following the scent of the raw meat we were carrying in plastic bags to cook like real explorers, with nothing more than a tinderbox and some newspaper. I don't remember whose idea it was; maybe I don't want to remember it was Max's. It wasn't mine, but I do know that it drew me in right away, like an electric current hooked directly to a node of curiosity and exhilaration. We gathered rocks and stones and piled them at the entrance to a cave, then we tossed in a piece of meat and whistled to the dog. It climbed inside easily and, while it was distracted by the meat, we closed the entrance behind it. The hole wasn't very big—it was round, like an eye socket, and when we put the last of the stones in place we set off running as fast as we could. There wasn't another sound. We were so frightened we exploded in a fit of laughter; when our laughter died down, we were left silent and ashamed. We didn't climb the Elephant that day. José Luis got on his bicycle, Max and I ran straight home. I don't know what the others did. None of us ever mentioned the dog again, not even me and Max, and none of us ever returned to that cave.

That was the same summer as the kiss, but I don't know which came first. Max and I were on the front porch of my house during the afternoon siesta, when we were forbidden to go down to the beach alone. He never talked about sad things, which fascinated me because sadness ran through him like air runs through air; I figured that was why he didn't bother to feel it, just like the air didn't need to breathe itself.

'You never cry?' I asked.

'I can't.'

'What do you mean, you can't?'

'Sometimes I make myself. I pinch myself until tears come out.'

'You're the weirdest person I know,' I said.

'I couldn't when my grandmother died, even.'

'Why didn't you pinch yourself?'

He shrugged. He looked out into the distance, toward the slope where people parked on their way to go fishing. The cicadas buzzed furiously. The sun made everything shimmer like a mirage, and the flashes of light reflecting off the car windows left green spots in my eyes. I held out my arm to Max.

'Show me how you do it,' I said. 'Pinch me.'

'I don't want to pinch you.'

'I'm asking you to. I want to cry for this plant that's dying of thirst.'

He glanced at the flower bed that separated my house from the gravel walkway. In it was a wilted bellflower with folded leaves and faded petals—some still a pale blue, but most yellowed and burned by the sun.

'You don't need help to cry. And what do you care about that plant?'

'I'm asking you to pinch me. If you're my friend, you'll do it. Are you my friend or not?' I offered him my hand again, and this time he took it.

'I am,' he said.

Before he pinched me, he warned me that he wasn't going to let go and that he was only doing it because we were friends. Deal, I said. My skin was dark and tight from all the salt, and the two white scars I had on my knees from an old bicycle accident were showing. Ready? he asked. Ready, I replied. Max dug his nails into me and I yelped; by reflex, I tried to pull my hand away but he wouldn't let go. He held tight and kept squeezing as he looked intently at me. My face had turned red—I could feel the heat in my cheeks and the cicadas buzzing in my ears—but I didn't cry. I was determined to make it to the end. It was like a staring contest, and Delfa had taught me that the secret of those was to think about something else. You could think, for example, about a penguin. You could think, for example, about a hummingbird. Max studied the moisture welling in my eyes, then eased his grip and looked down.

'That's enough,' he said, and let go.

His nails had left throbbing dents in my skin.

'You let go before I cried,' I said.

Then he leaned forward and kissed me with firm, closed lips. That was it. We didn't touch each other again for five years. I'd never kissed anyone before, but I couldn't say that because a second later Max was howling with laughter.

'Your face!' he said. 'You should have seen your face.'

'What face? What about my face?'

Max couldn't speak, he pressed his forearms to his stomach as he choked on his laughter. He'd let himself fall backward onto the hot tiles of the porch.

'Your face . . . Your face . . .' was all he managed to say.

'Stupid!' I laughed, having caught his fit. 'Look at you! You're the one crying now.'

That face, the one he said he'd seen when he dug his nails into me, appeared to Max in a hallucination the first night he ate sacred medicine. More than twenty-five years had passed since that beginning swathed in the sound of cicadas, and we were already feeling the end draw near. The shaman blew into his hand, Max said, and he saw a serpent. It was shedding its skin, which melted from it the way paper wrinkles fine and dark as it burns. Max spent two days in a tent with stones that turned the air so hot he had to press his nose to the earth so he didn't suffocate. We breathed earth, he said, and there was oxygen there. I don't know if the plant was still active in him when he came home. He seemed like a different person. Calm and at the same time euphoric, though it was a contained euphoria. He told me that in his vision the serpent opened its mouth and there was something inside.

'A fetus was coming out of the serpent's mouth,' he said, 'and I knew the birth was killing it.'

What emerged from the serpent's mouth was a woman who had my face—*that* face, the one he'd seen all those years ago—but who was also a monster.

'You're the wrapping,' he said, 'but something else lies beneath. That face. A girl disguised as a monster.'

'Or a monster disguised as a girl?'

'Does it matter?' he asked.

'It matters to me.'

'The monster and the girl were one.'

In the end, the sandcastle crumbles.

It does.

You know that, you *always* knew. So why did you build it?

You tell me.

Not for it to last, not to protect it from the waves.

I see where you're going with this.

The journey isn't a journey if it isn't dense with paradox.

Days passed from one blackout to the next with no word from my mother. It's hard for me to describe time in confinement, because if anything characterized those periods it was the sensation of existing in a kind of non-time. We lived in a constant state of anticipation, but we weren't waiting for anything in particular. We just waited. And what we were hoping would happen was nothing, because any change might be for the worse. As long as everything stayed still, I could linger in the non-time of memory. Mauro had watched me call my mother so often he'd begun to think of it as a game; he even started picking up the phone and having conversations in his invented language. Sometimes I dialed my mother's number and let him stand there with the handset to his ear, listening as the rings echoed on the other end of the line. After a while he'd get bored and pass me the phone.

'Hello no,' he'd say.

The blackouts made our confinement—that porous time skidding across itself—even worse. I say *porous* because thoughts clung to it, looping like the cassettes Max and I used to play backward in my room with the door closed because listening to tapes backward was another thing the adults would forbid without explanation. We were looking for the hidden message. *Egassem neddih eht rof gnikool erew ew*. Eventually the tape would get tangled, and we'd end up taking the cassette apart, seeking answers to the mystery deep in the device itself, in the physical dimension of things.

It was Wednesday or Thursday. It was Friday or Saturday. It didn't matter what day it was, what time it was, whether it was winter or spring. What mattered was the dense fog or the clouds forming in scarlet threads; what mattered was the numbing silence or the alarm announcing a wind. I had learned to read the clouds, learned to mistrust a clear day. I hadn't heard from my mother in almost two weeks. I lay on the couch to leaf through one of her books but didn't get past the first few pages. I searched for notes in the margins, some kind of clue about her, the things she cared about, the things that hurt her. Who was she when she wasn't with me? How did she play her other roles of neighbor, friend, lover?

Around the same time Delfa showed up in a wig, my mother began going out with men. She never introduced me to any of them formally, but I'd open the door for them when they came to pick her up, or run out to the car to take my mother something she'd forgotten. They said hello but never fawned over me. The men who interested her were pretty similar to one another, and for a while I was convinced they were all the same person: gray, quiet, tough. My mother associated masculinity with silence, or at least with a lack of verbosity. She, on the other hand, was a loud, lively figure who dazzled us all. I once heard her say that she wanted to give herself a chance.

Delfa began to stay with me when my mother went out at night. We would eat in front of the television, watching dubbed movies or a quiz show called *Dare to Dream*. In the blue glow of the television I'd rest my head on Delfa's lap and she'd run her fingers through my hair. I'd struggle to resist the spell, the drowsiness that washed over me as she untangled my hair, because I wanted to be awake with her, not to fall asleep and open my eyes after she'd gone. Delfa asked me once what I dared to dream of. By then Max already occupied most of my thoughts, but I didn't tell Delfa that. I said I dreamed that she and I could go live in a house at the top of a tall tree and never have to work again. She laughed and said: That sounds lovely. Without my mother, I said, so she can't make me do chores. I make you do chores, too, she replied. Yeah, but not as many. Delfa would send me to bed when a little mouse in pajamas came on the television to wish all the children sweet dreams. I would never be tired at that hour and would toss and turn in the faint light from the living room, where Delfa would still be watching television with the volume down. I would pretend to be asleep whenever she came to check on me, but even with my eyes closed I could sense her mass in the doorway. At some point, I'd hear the jangling of my mother's keys, and the next morning I'd find a playbill on the living room table, a napkin with a restaurant logo, souvenirs from a party, Brazilian candy wrappers.

My mother eventually stopped going out at night. By then I was a teenager and didn't care if she got in late. I heard her tell a friend over the phone that she hadn't found what she was looking for, but I never understood if she'd been looking badly, searching in all the wrong corners, or if what she was looking for simply didn't exist. I never heard of her dating anyone again, and over time that part of her life went quiet. Her desire was no longer tied to the attention one strange man after another had showered on her for as long as I could remember; it had shifted to me, to her role as a mother. I had suddenly become the center of her world—I never knew how or why. The decision certainly had nothing to do with me. I don't think my mother ever once suffered over love. She enjoyed feeling admired, she enjoyed the little gestures, the frivolities of pleasure, but she could live without them; that was her greatest discovery.

Mauro walked over to ask me if it was his birthday. He'd been obsessed with his birthday ever since I made him that cardboard hat.

'No,' I said, 'but you can wear your hat.'

He took it down from the television set and put it on. The elastic was dead, but it managed to keep the hat in place, pulled taut between his chins.

'Is my birthday?'

'I already told you it's not.'

I wonder why I didn't lie to him. Hadn't it stopped mattering whether it was Monday or Tuesday, whether it was three or six o'clock? We could celebrate every day, I could sing him Happy Birthday, we could invent a new time. But instead I insisted on *the truth*.

'Light no,' said Mauro.

'It will come back soon.'

'Now?'

'Later. Before nighttime.'

I suggested we play Find the Sun, another of his favorite games.

'Okay, Mauro, where's the sun?'

He walked over to the window, pressed his sticky hands to the glass, and peered at the sky. He was looking for a pale blotch, a spot of liquid mercury. It wasn't always easy: the white ball might be hidden behind the trees in the plaza, or the fog might be too thick for the sun to bore through with its solitary eye. Sometimes he couldn't find it, or he confused it with the smaller, brighter light of a crane down by the port, or he pointed at some faint image moving in the distance, a sluggish glow, maybe the lights of an army helicopter up in the second or third ring. When that happened, he'd fog the window with his breath and draw pictures with his finger.

'Sun there,' said Mauro, pointing at a whitish hollow in the sky. It looked as if the clouds might escape through it.

'Very good!' I said, applauding. 'You found it.'

He clapped, too. Then he pointed to the trees in the plaza.

'Bird.'

My whole body tensed. I searched the boughs of the evergreens and the branches of the other trees that, half-bare, revealed an equestrian statue. In another era, the dark horse had always been covered in pigeon droppings.

'Birds don't live there, Mauro.'

'Where are they?'

'Out where your mom lives. Do you see birds when you're there?'

'No,' he said, hanging his head as if he'd just spoken the saddest words in the world. 'They're sleeping.' Just then we heard an electric hum and the lamp next to the television lit up.

'Light!' shouted Mauro, giving a little hop. He ran in circles in front of the television, always on the verge of slipping on the rug or bumping into the lamp. 'Lightlightlight!'

He ran blindly, his hair covering his eyes like a woolly mammoth.

'Come over here,' I said, laughing softly. 'Let's do something with that hair.'

I will be cutting Mauro's hair when the phone rings. He'll have a towel around his neck and his locks will be damp and stretch downward, the right half cut shorter than the left, where his hair will fall dark and stiff to his shoulder.

'Don't move, I have a phone call,' I'll say to him.

'Hello? Are you there, dear?'

The urgency in my mother's voice is enough to tell me that something bad has happened.

'Valdivia's in the hospital. They came to get him and now the store is cordoned off with yellow tape.' She will say this and then burst into tears.

'I've been calling you for two weeks, Mom. Where were you? Why didn't you pick up?'

Mauro will feel my tension and will lift his head to look up at me. I'll signal him with my eyes that everything's fine.

'They came for Valdivia!' she will say, between sobs.

'Try to calm down a little.'

'Can't you see what's happening?'

'We'll find another store, Mom.'

'It's not that.'

'Do you have power there? It's been less than an hour since ours came back on, and the lights are already flickering.'

'Power? Who cares? Oh, it's all just too terrible . . .'

I will hear nothing but her sobs for a while; I'll think about the patrol vans gathering bodies, probably the same ones they saved from suicide the week before. My mother isn't crying over the store, she's crying because she'd thought she was safe in her foggy enclave and now the illness has broken through her little fence of delusion.

'What does the schoolteacher say?'

'She wants to leave. The agronomist asked her to go inland with him.'

'With her piano and everything?'

'It's the inlanders who are behind this whole thing. They wanted to get rid of Valdivia. They're a mafia, dear. They have a whole black market set up. The inlanders got rid of him.'

Mauro will slide off the bench, take the towel from his neck, and play with it like a bullfighter's cape. *Olé!* he'll say, between pivots. He will spin around several times, then get dizzy and crash against the wall.

'Careful, Mauro.'

'They want to corner the market.'

'Where did you hear that?'

'The agronomist. He has contacts, he knows.'

When next I look over, Mauro will be in the kitchen, sitting on the floor and digging around in the trash. He'll be eating a lettuce heart, but I won't have the energy to scold him, to take more food from his mouth. I will think: It's only lettuce.

'We'll find another store until Valdivia gets back.'

'Where?'

'I'll bring provisions soon. Don't worry.'

'No, stay inside. Can't you see what it's like out there? Oh, when will it end?'

El Príncipe had brought a red wind so strong it had started to reach the inland cities. The panic it was causing had led to riots and evacuations. The drone cameras on the news showed caravans of cars trying to evacuate along the highway going north.

'Just try to calm down . . .'

I will think fast, feeling my brain quiver as it weighs options. Part of me will want to berate her, to tell her I'd thought she was dead, but the more sensible and resigned part will hold me back. Talking with my mother was like approaching a wild animal; she could easily feel cornered and lash out again.

'I'll come spend a few days with you after they pick Mauro up,' I will say. 'They'll be here soon.'

She won't hear me. She will have entered that state of panic where monologue seems like the only viable defense.

'What will become of Valdivia, dear? What will become of us?'

That night, Mauro and I stayed up late watching television. They were airing the midday news again: images of unruly crowds in face masks, respirators. It was the first time the wind threatened a city deep inland.

'We sold everything to come here,' a woman sobbed into the camera. 'And now this.'

'They're gonna keep pushing us north until we fall off the edge of the country,' grumbled someone else.

People lined up at the supermarkets and gas stations. There was no water, no purification tablets; the supermarket shelves were empty except for the little cups of Meatrite stacked high in huge refrigerators. They were about to find out what it's like. To have that smell imprinted on your nostrils, that gritty texture eroding your tongue. Meatrite was the new processing plant's star product, and the inlanders avoided it whenever they could. An ideal foodstuff: twenty grams of protein per portion, served in a small plastic cup. The plant opened its maw and spat out pink slime; those little cups glided along the tongue of its conveyor belts and fell, lovely and well designed, into our laps. We all hated the new plant, but we relied on it and therefore owed it our gratitude. A good mother, one who provided for us. And there we were, choking on our rage like a bunch of teenagers who hate their parents but owe them everything. I brought you into this world, I gave you life, my mother would say to me, and I would immediately feel the weight of an enormous debt, an invisible sack of coins I was supposed to carry around forever. That's what we are when we're born: meat paste gasping for air, little balls of pink slime that, once we're pushed out, have no choice but to agglutinate to that other body, the mother's, biting down hard on the teat of life. But no. I'm being unfair. Not all children hate the hand that shields and scars them. Some don't. I've even met a few of them. And so I guess there must also be people who love the national meat-processing plant, people who feel proud of it and who would forgive it anything.

No one knew how long El Príncipe was going to last. A panel of experts was arguing about it on set. There was a famous writer, a windbag who had been catapulted to fame by a pulpy adventure novel; there was also a marine biologist, the leader of the health workers union, and a man with thick glasses and a beard I knew from the agency. He had a stutter and arrived just as I was on my way out; now there he was, sitting on that little couch with his legs splayed like some kind of magnate. The problem, someone said, is the government's arrogance. They didn't do a sweep when they had the chance, added someone else. Mauro had fallen asleep in my arms and his weight on my leg was giving me pins and needles. Every now and then a shudder ran through his body. Did he feel hunger in his dreams?

'Since when is it my job to save every lunatic wandering around out there?'

The man with the beard was gesticulating with one hand and stroking his microphone cable with the other. The biologist stared at him in horror.

'Not everyone stayed because they wanted to,' she said.

Mauro's body jerked again. *Shhhh*, I said. I turned the volume down and watched the bearded man gesticulate silently. He spoke with the conviction of someone who had risen through the ranks as a journalist for the State. He'd probably started out like me, writing filler pieces meant to distract people from what was happening. When I left, the agency had recently been awarded a contract with the new Ministry. We wrote content for *The Good Life*, optimistic articles about how well the river drainage and the upgrades at Clinics were going, recommendations for safety protocols, success stories from the migration inland. The guy might have been a charlatan, but at least he was dedicated. I, on the other hand, as I told my boss the day I quit, had no faith in what we were doing. Not surprisingly, she didn't try to stop me from walking out. There were dozens of bearded men waiting to take my place, each one armed with the tools required for gilding reality. You don't believe the world's stories deserve to be told, she had said to me in her office. We'd been classmates at university and I guess I should have been grateful for the opportunity. Maybe, I replied. Or maybe the problem is that there's no one to tell them to.

I slid off the couch, covered Mauro with a blanket, and left him sleeping there. I didn't want to wake him up and it would have been impossible for me to carry him to bed. I glanced back at him from the doorway to my room. The glow of the sky was so intense that night it looked like his motionless body was being warmed by an infrared lamp.

A cloud is a cloud no matter how far it is from the ground.

When I opened my eyes the next morning, Mauro was leaning over me. The night had done nothing to ease my exhaustion, which I felt as soon as I tried to move: a force of gravity pulling me down into the mattress. I could have shattered into so many pieces no one would've been able to put me back together. The feeling reminded me of those chocolates people used to buy in Bariloche: big, fragile curls that crumbled between your fingers. There were still seven days left before they came for Mauro, and during the final stretch I always woke up feeling like I couldn't breathe. I performed my tasks mechanically, like a worker in a poultry plant; I dressed and undressed him, cut his nails, ran a sponge along the folds of his adipose anatomy. Sometimes I pictured myself taking an overnight bus, reclining my sleeper seat, closing my eyes, and waking up in another country. Sometimes I pictured myself digging a long, deep tunnel to another land. But all my escape routes led me back to Max, like those circular highway exits that spit you back out right where you started. I thought about the money in my safe. One of those days, they'd come back from the countryside to find my apartment empty; I'd be gone, and so would my roll of bills. Mauro's mother would deposit him on my doorstep like a potato, like a bud unable to flower. But I would be far away, on the other side of the country, on the other side of the night.

'Is it day?' asked Mauro, standing beside my bed. The pillow had marked deep lines in his cheek. It was day, but the light couldn't push its way through, like on those afternoons that suddenly turn nocturnal, cast into darkness by menacing clouds. Still muddled by sleep, I looked over at the window. The fog had finally returned, which at least meant the wind had died down. A truce, however brief.

'What time is it?' I asked.

'Day.'

I turned on the lamp next to my bed. My mood was a wagon or a plow I needed to push from the moment I got up. Seven days could be an eternity, but not in the sense of that platitude about the life span of seven moths. I had to write about that once, the ten animals with the shortest life expectancy. It was one of the first pieces the agency had assigned me. Butterflies lived for between one and six weeks; bees only four, just a little longer than flies. One insect, with a transparent body and huge lentil eyes, lived for less than a day: the ephemeral mayfly. No, it wasn't that kind of eternity. It was like being forced to walk for seven days straight, your blisters oozing their warm liquid, your shoes opening the same wound over and over.

I went over to the window and Mauro stood on tiptoe beside me. We stared at the unvaried gray landscape: cupolas, television antennas, water tanks, old bare clotheslines, the useless cranes by the docks. I looked at the cranes, lit by equally useless bulbs, and remembered reading somewhere about a man who dreamed about a garden full of giraffes.

'It's going to rain,' I said.

I said it just like that, casually, even though I knew it was impossible. Whatever might come out of those clouds, it wasn't going to be water accumulated in the sky. It hadn't rained in a long time; I'm sure Mauro couldn't remember the last time. I didn't either, come to think of it. The last rain had been completely unmemorable. There were no broken umbrellas, no flooding sewers, no leaking roofs. Last times are always like that. All I remember is that a little while later the fish washed up on shore.

The last time I saw Max outside the hospital, I didn't know it was going to be the last, either. I'd taken a regional bus to Villa del Rosario that morning. It was overcast and piercingly cold, the way it gets on days without wind. Max's new house, his bachelor pad, was still half-finished and had the fanciful, ramshackle air of amateur architecture. He had decided to move to the coast, the most dangerous part of the country, because he'd gotten a lead on this house through one of his friends from the plant rituals. I got off the bus and headed for the street behind his, where trees grew in an empty lot. He wasn't expecting me. I walked across the damp, silent carpet of pine needles. From there I could see his house and patio, his grill, the colorful clips on his clotheslines. I didn't have to wait long before he came outside. Even in the cold, Max couldn't stand being stuck indoors. I watched him carry logs back and forth. A little cloud left his warm body with each breath. He was wearing a blue V-neck sweater that, if it wasn't the exact one he always wore, probably had just as many moth holes and cigarette burns. His neck was bare and he grasped the rough bark of the logs with his dry hands.

He'd always had contempt for pain, even before his first attempts to tame his body. As if you could separate the two, I'd tell him; this was just the visible part of who he was. He could walk on burrs, bear the itch of mosquito bites without scratching, sit motionless under the sun until his shoulders burned to a crisp. Later, his back would peel and I would lift the layers of transparent skin to reveal another one, newer and more red, beneath. I would say: You realize that this skin has never touched air? My fingers, my own skin, were its first contact.

Max left the wood inside and came back out to sit on one of the benches near the grill. He smoked languidly, like a prematurely old teenager. If he really did have powers, he must have known I was spying on him from the empty lot; he must have been putting on a show for me. He always put on a show for women. He had even wanted to be an actor for a while. He went on auditions and everything, and he landed a role in a movie. They gave him a scene where he sat in a parked car on a rainy night. Then he quit, like he quit everything he started; he often talked about these former passions with disdain. One day I'd walked in on him watching the movie. It was still light outside, but he'd closed the blinds in our room and the television glowed in a cloud of smoke. He was watching himself with that crooked half smile on his face.

'Look at that,' he'd said, his eyes glued to his own image. 'I used to want to be everyone, now I want to be no one.'

Max finished his cigarette and crushed it out on the table. He tossed the butt into the grill and stared off into the distance as the fog condensed into droplets, which soaked noiselessly into the ground. I let the eucalyptus pods I'd been gathering in my palm fall to the carpet of moist pine needles. My glove smelled like mint. What's that paradox about how you can't surrender without first letting go, but letting go is impossible until you've surrendered? Max could let go of everything, even compassion for himself; I, on the other hand, felt like a prehistoric octopus clinging to everything I once had. Why was Max any harder to let go of than those eucalyptus pods? There is a tick in the forests of Switzerland that causes a sudden and fatal encephalitis. The life expectancy of Inuit people is fifteen years lower than that of other residents of Canada. Exposure to air and light oxidizes meat, which is why it is cured with sodium nitrate. I knew all this from my job at the agency, where day after day my head filled with useless facts.

I suddenly lost hope. I don't know what I had expected to happen, what mysterious alchemy I'd been hoping for, but I suddenly had no idea why I'd gone all the way out there or what I was doing behind that tree. That was when I decided to quit my job at the agency and accept the offer Mauro's parents had made. At first, they'd asked me to go inland with them, said they would set me up with a little house in Once de Octubre, a new town thirty kilometers from their property, but I declined. There was too much tying me to the city. This is my home, I had said, there's room for him here. A few days later, they brought Mauro to me. His mother handed him off along with several boxes of food that filled my cupboards. Their suitcases were packed and waiting in the SUV that idled in the garage. Was that before or after the last rain? My building was still half-full then; the elevator still went up and down with its hippopotamus wheeze. For those who stayed, the people who left had succumbed to the panic being spread on television. I remember how relieved I felt when she said goodbye and I was left alone with Mauro, as if he were the portal to a better world. I repeated the same thing to myself, over and over: that nothing tied me to him and, soon, nothing would tie me to Max; that in just a few months I would save up enough cash to move to Brazil.

I let Mauro eat his breakfast in the living room, in front of the television. For the first time in weeks, the Department of Meteorology had announced a low risk of wind. From the kitchen, I could hear Mauro mumbling at the screen. What does it mean, what does it mean, asked the muffled voices on the show. Measuring air particles. Says who? Says me. Who are you? Raucous laughter, but canned: a whole stadium laughing. The program was trashy, but anything was better than the silence of the fog. I found some plastic bags and started filling them with rice, lentils, and garbanzos—the legumes that would save the nation, according to the agronomist. From the top shelf I grabbed a few containers of milk and packages of bow-tie pasta. They'd been up there so long they were covered in dust. I wiped them clean and stuffed everything into a garbage bag. A packet of cookies, a jar of dulce de leche, a box of frozen hamburger patties, two cans of corn. I left out the cups of Meatrite because my mother found it disgusting. She fought about it with Valdivia once. He hated it when people criticized his products; he believed he was performing a vital function in the neighborhood, and whenever the wind would delay a shipment he would say things like: I can't starve the town to death. It's a disgrace, my mother would say, it's regurgitated food. But even regurgitated food could be sustenance.

There wasn't much left when I was done, but it would be enough

to get us through this final week, and I still had our emergency provisions. On the way back I could ask the taxi to stop at an underground
market in the neighborhood. The drivers knew the transformed city
better than anyone, better than the police patrols; they knew the illegal shops that cropped up like mushrooms and then shut right back
down, where a box of hamburger patties could cost up to a thousand pesos; they knew the guys who could forge you a certificate of
health and help you cross the border, and how to get into the black
markets where they sold gas, spare parts, air filters, water-purifying
tablets. I opened the refrigerator, poured myself a glass of milk, and
drank it in one gulp. There was barely any fresh food left. For that,
we'd have to wait until the driver brought us a new box of colorless,
worm-ridden fruits and vegetables with strange malformations but
no risk of disease.

Mauro was still sitting transfixed in front of the television. I
walked behind him and touched his head. No! he cried, jerking
away. Then he asked me if it was his birthday. I'll let you know
when, I said. I didn't have time to look for a taxi outside, so I
dialed the number of the official service. The line was busy, and
I spent several minutes pressing redial until I finally got through.
The automated voice, honeyed and overly warm, said what it always did: *For medical transport, press one. If you are near the coast but
do not need medical transport, press two. For services inland, press three.*
I pressed two and landed right back at the recording with elevator
music: *For medical transport, press one.* I circled around the maze of
options leading nowhere for a while before deciding to press one.
The operator answered right away. She already had my address and
phone number, but she asked for them again; after confirming my

identity, she requested the name and ID number of the infected individual.

'No one's infected,' I said. 'I just need a taxi.'

'This option is for medical transport only.'

Before she could hang up on me, I told her that option two wasn't working. The operator, whose voice in no way resembled the velvety tones of the recorded greeting, told me that all other services were suspended due to the storm.

'Medical transport only,' she said again.

'Are you saying there's no taxis?'

Like a trained parrot, she repeated, 'Medical transport only.'

'Is it because of El Príncipe? But they just announced low risk of wind on the news.'

'It's a question of safety, ma'am.'

'You're telling me there's not a single taxi in the whole city?'

'It's for the protection of the drivers, ma'am.'

'I can pay the contaminant fee,' I said.

The operator fell silent, and the silence filled with static.

'Official taxis are not running, ma'am.'

That was her way of telling me I could take a private cab, illegal rides that negotiated their fees on the spot. For a woman carrying cash, getting into one of those cabs was practically suicide. But I didn't get the chance to reply; the operator was already running the union's automated recording: *Call ahead to ride safe.*

I walked over to the window and looked for the sun, like Mauro had done so many times before, but couldn't even make out the trees in the plaza. It was like trying to see through layers of dirty glass; if a spot of color managed to pass through one, it got trapped by the next. You had to trust the fog, to close your mind to all the dangers you were exposing yourself to and use it as camouflage. You had to sink into its protective embrace. In the kitchen, I made sure the refrigerator was locked and the trash closed up. I removed the bag from the bin. Mauro heard me and came to see what was going on; he was barefoot and still in his pajamas, chewing on the wooden stick that had once held a kind of chicken nugget they marketed as health food but which was really just another artificially flavored meat by-product.

'I'm going out to buy food,' I said. 'Be good and don't touch anything. Promise?'

He said no; he didn't want me to leave him alone in the apartment, something I'd never done in all the time he'd lived with me.

'I'm hungry,' he said.

'It's not time to eat, Mauro. You just ate your nugget and an ice cream.'

'I'm hungry,' he insisted. And I believed him, but I needed to pretend I didn't. I needed to wait out his tantrums without guilt. That was my job: to watch him get fatter and fatter, and eventually (when?) to watch him die without feeling the pain a mother would.

Mauro said again that he didn't want to be left alone. He squinted his eyes as if he were crying, but all that came out of him was a gagging sound. Then he threw the stick he'd been chewing on, ran into his room, and slammed the door. I could hear him screaming No! No! in there. When I opened the door, I saw him lying in bed with his pillow pressed between his knees and three fingers in his mouth.

'Mauro, come here.'

He shook his head no as he tried to get his whole hand into his mouth, spit dribbling down his chin.

'Don't make me count to three . . .' And I did start counting, to myself, but was interrupted by the image of Mauro digging his teeth into his own flesh. 'Take your hand out of there, or I'll have to give you a time-out.'

I sometimes wondered if he could really go that far, if he could really devour his own fingers, drink his own blood. What would the syndrome do, if left to its own devices? Mauro's brain would never say *enough*. Rotten eggs, mold, plaster; he could eat until he choked, until he shredded his esophagus like an old rag.

'Come over here, I have something for you.'

Mauro grudgingly followed me into the living room and stopped in front of the television, watching me. I found the bag of candies on the top shelf of the kitchen cabinets and grabbed a handful.

'Look, you can pick. What color do you want?'

He approached me with one finger still in his mouth, like an old bone, and peered intently at my outstretched hand. All those colors. Candies you had to work on for half an hour before they were soft enough to chew.

'Reds.'

'Okay, take all the reds.'

He started picking them out one by one, careful not to miss any. When he was done, I tossed the rest back in the bag and locked the cabinet. He asked me how long I'd be gone.

'I'll be back before you finish those candies.'

I put on my coat; as I slipped my hand into the pocket, I felt a lump and the rough texture of paper towels. My mother's scones. They'd been there since my last visit and were hard as rocks. My life had been on pause since then, like a toy without batteries. I could have given the old scones to Mauro, let him gnaw on them, soak them in saliva until they softened. But no. I left the apartment with the bag of provisions in one hand and a bag of trash in the other. As I turned the key in the lock, I could hear Mauro repeating my name.

My mother says that when I was three or four years old, I used to cry every time she went to work. She says that one time I grabbed her ankles to try to keep her from leaving, that she dragged me all the way to the elevator. She says that another time, I asked her to marry me. I don't remember any of that. I remember Delfa letting me make little sausages with the extra dough when she made pastel de fiambre, and cutting out dresses for my paper dolls with me, letting me brush her wig while she sat on the couch with her mending, nearly bald, just a few dark hairs scattered around her scalp that were nothing like the ash blond I'd always known. Or playing Mikado together, her fingers too fat to pick up a stick without moving the rest, or how she'd get angry when I locked myself in my room to listen to cassettes. But I never told my mother; I never confessed that I don't remember a single thing from those years when she was supposedly the center of my world.

That's impossible.

Why?

Because there's only one center.

But there are many worlds.

A beat-up black car circled the plaza; it was the only thing moving. I crossed the street and threw the bag of trash onto a mound of plastic that had been compressing and hardening in the moist air. The black car flashed its lights at me. I didn't respond and let it pass by, but the driver stopped on the corner and leaned across the passenger seat to roll the window down. I walked over to test the waters: an old man with knotty hands and dark spots on his face. He seemed harmless, but no one was harmless these days.

'Where can I take you?'

'To Los Pozos,' I said. 'How much?'

'Four hundred. It's a good deal.'

He could have named any price, but even so, he seemed nervous. In this strange transaction of needs and fears, I had far more to lose; the important thing was not letting it show.

'Two. That's all I have.'

'Two hundred doesn't even cover the gas,' he said, resting his hands on the wheel. The button on his sleeve was missing and I could see a sliver of his frail wrist, two sharp bones pressed against skin that was so thin and dry it was nearly transparent. This might have been his first fare, the first time he risked what little he had left to buy gas on the black market and start up as a private cab.

'Four hundred if you wait for me and then take me to Clinics,' I said.

The old man did a few calculations and flashed me a row of small, yellow teeth. I sat in the front seat and slid the bag of food between my legs. The dense, dull fog parted as we drove through it, slicing the darkness in two.

'Looks like rain,' I said, and immediately felt myself flush with embarrassment. So naive, as if the old man's presence had suddenly turned me into a child. 'I mean, that would be something, right?'

'It's nice, the smell of rain,' he said.

'It is.'

'And the sound of it. Especially in the summer. Best time for making fry bread.'

His gaunt cheeks folded like an accordion when he smiled. He drove with his torso angled over the wheel, peering into the gap in the fog.

'I mean, I don't make it anymore. Got a lazy stomach these days. But back then . . .'

'And watermelon,' I said. 'A good sweet one.'

'Or a slice of pastafrola. Would you believe, last night I dreamed I was eating an empanada. Heaps of real meat, well seasoned. Not like the ones you get now.'

'Meatrite,' I said. '*Meat for all.*'

'It was so real in my dream I could smell it.'

We fell silent. After a while, he blurted out, 'Doesn't cost anything to dream.'

He told me that before the epidemic he'd had a stall at the Sunday market where he sold pets. Canaries and ornamental fish. That's what he called them: ornamental. What happened to all those fish that lived in aquariums? I didn't ask him, but I did think back to when Delfa and I used to go to that market. I'd help her carry the shopping bags and always looked forward to the moment we reached the animal stalls. I'd stare at the rabbits, all huddled together, and the goldfish trailing their delicate veils among bubbles and castles and treasure chests.

'It was nice work,' said the old man, 'but tough. Kids were always poking their fingers in the cages, getting the animals sick. But when those canaries would sing early in the morning, that sure was nice. I'd take my yerba mate out in the yard and listen to them. Then I'd go cage by cage, cutting their nails. I made sure never to get near the vein. They stop singing right away when they're sick. I noticed they were looking kind of shaky a while before the first storm. Then the diarrhea started and their feet swelled up.'

'What happened to them?'

'What do you think?' he said, and that seemed to end the conversation. He asked me who I was going to see at Clinics and I told him about Max.

'He's in chronic care.'

The old man glanced at me; it was only a second, but it was enough to recognize the wistful look I'd seen in so many eyes before.

'He hit the jackpot,' he said.

'We're divorced.'

'Kids?'

I shook my head.

He had a daughter in critical care and a granddaughter inland.

'Boarding schools are getting more expensive by the day,' he said. 'And harder to get into. You have no idea what people are willing to do to send their kids there.'

I didn't, but I could imagine. I could also imagine the scrawny old man negotiating with mercenaries selling gas on the black market and chewing dry seeds, trying to save every last peso. Did they sell canaries on the black market, too? Ornamental fish? I couldn't bring myself to ask him that, either.

'Have you ever heard of the butterfly paradox?'

'Sweetheart, my head's foggier than this here street. Go easy on me.'

'The caterpillar, while it's busy being a caterpillar, can't be a butterfly.'

The old man's face took on a serious expression.

'Okay, explain it to me,' he said after a while.

'It's a paradox. You understand it and you don't.'

'You understand something *or* you don't. They taught me that much in school.'

'Then a paradox is something you don't understand,' I said, but I wasn't so sure anymore and wished I could ask Max. 'At least, it's not something you understand with your mind.'

We arrived in Los Pozos and parked in front of my mother's house. I had a terrible feeling. The fog pressed in through the open windows like a serpent eating its tail. I knocked but no one answered, and I heard no movement inside. The whole neighborhood had gone silent. I stuck my head in through one of the windows and saw my mother on the sofa: arms crossed loose over her belly, mouth hanging open, thin hair fanning across half of her face, a book propped against her legs. I tried the doorknob. The door wasn't locked, and when I opened it she gave a start that sent her book tumbling to the floor.

'Don't fall asleep with the windows open,' I said. 'Can't you see this weather isn't normal?'

'How did you get here?' she asked, disoriented.

She was a mess; her face was all puffy and her robe looked like an old bedspread.

'There are no taxis. No one will say what's going on.'

She leaned forward and touched her shins.

'I fell asleep.'

'Yeah, inside a cloud. You looked like a little angel. Is that what heaven's like?'

'Could be worse.'

She struggled to her feet and came over to see what I was doing.

'Where did you get all that?'

I laid the provisions out on the table. I thought I saw her glance approvingly at me, but in retrospect I'm not so sure.

'Mauro's parents will arrive in a few days. Have you heard anything about Valdivia?'

'Not a word.'

She walked over to the window that looked onto the backyard and closed it.

'Everyone is leaving. Marcela says she doesn't want to leave me here alone, but the agronomist is building her a little house inland.'

She walked around closing the windows one by one, trapping the fog inside with us.

'She's insisting I go along.'

'You should listen to her.'

When she reached the window facing the street, she lingered for a while, looking out. It was hard to recognize her like that. The outline of her broad frame against the light. The vanity she had shed like dead skin.

'Whose car is that?' she asked.

'I can't stay long. Mauro's home alone.'

'He's old enough.'

'You don't know what he's capable of. He could cut his finger off and not even notice.'

'He's lucky, then.'

'What are you talking about, Mom? Could you try for just a minute to put yourself in someone else's shoes?'

She was still at the window with her back to me, in that robe faded from so much washing.

'There you go again, aggressive and irritable. You won't go far like that.'

'I don't want to go anywhere.'

She nodded, in silence.

'Why don't you accept Marcela's invitation? She's going to need an audience out there. Or do you think the agronomist is going to listen to her play the piano?'

My mother shrugged, drawn to the old man's car like a magnet, to its promise of escape.

'She was one of those who said they'll die in Los Pozos, and now look.'

'Why don't you go with her?'

'I don't know,' she said. 'They've got the plant running at half capacity until the storm passes. They can't transport the animals. When do you think the storm will pass?'

'If it does.'

'They're certain it will. I mean, can you imagine? All that money they've invested, for nothing.'

'It's immoral,' I said.

'It's just wasted money, that's all. They're caught between a rock and a hard place, that's why they go around pressuring people like Valdivia.'

'Marcela told you that?'

'She plays dumb. But come quick, look at this.'

She waved me over to the window.

'Speak of the Devil.'

Across the street, the schoolteacher was talking to a man with a leather briefcase.

'That's the agronomist.'

We laughed. His German respirator made him look like he was wearing a ski mask with his business suit. It was an old-fashioned suit: pants cut too wide and creased too sharply, square-cut blazer with shoulder pads.

'We're all in the hands of that eyesore,' I said.

The schoolteacher was in a white dressing gown with lace accents; she looked like a little girl from another century on the way to her First Communion.

'He has a driver,' said my mother as we watched a big, fancy car stop next to them. 'He brings her provisions from inland, but he charges her what we pay here. Can you believe that? He makes a profit, even with her.'

There was rage in her voice, as if the agronomist was responsible for the life we were living.

'Charges her for every last grain of rice.'

The man set his briefcase on the back seat and got in beside the driver. The schoolteacher waved goodbye until the car turned the corner, then she hurried inside.

'Poor Marcela,' said my mother. 'We're going to be up to our ears in that Meatrite crap. And you? How long until you've saved up enough?'

'Not long. A few months.'

'A few months. You say that like it's not a lifetime. It's the child, isn't it?'

'I'm saving up. I almost have enough.'

'You're sacrificing yourself for nothing. You're not his mother, you know.'

'I have to go. We can talk later.'

My mother walked over to the television and turned it on, ignoring what I'd just said to her. It was a huge unit, and it rested on a kind of cart, like a geriatric walker with little wheels.

'Did you hear about this lunatic?' she asked. On the screen was an image of one of the State's biologists. Saavedra, or Saravia. 'They're sending him to an asylum. He came up with this whole story about how the algae isn't algae, it's tiny organisms or something . . . Can you believe it?'

'I saw the news this morning.'

'Mental health is no laughing matter. But there are plenty of crazies out there who'll buy into his nonsense.'

'Do you remember the rabbit you gave me once?' I asked.

'What rabbit?'

'The rabbit. It was Delfa's idea.'

'It was *my* idea. Worst one I ever had.' She leaned over and turned up the volume on the television. 'Look at that. They're going to pay him a pension for the rest of his life.'

'I have to go, Mom.'

'Fine, fine,' she said, irritated, waving her hand as if she were shooing away a fly. 'Go on, go ahead.'

She turned off the television, but continued to stare at the black screen, or maybe at her reflection in its convex surface. I headed for the front door but changed my mind before I turned the knob. I went back into the living room. I took out my bundle of cash and removed enough for the taxi.

'Here,' I said. 'If Marcela offers, use this to buy food from the agronomist. Pay him whatever he's asking.'

'I'd rather die,' she sniffed, shaking her head and trying not to look at the money I'd left on the table so she wouldn't be tempted to count it.

'There are faster ways to go than by pride,' I said.

'You think I can't get what I need on my own? That I'm going to ask that mafioso, that slug, for favors? When did you ever want for anything?'

'I was calling you for two weeks. I thought you were dead.'

'Serves you right,' she said. 'What can I tell you.'

'Please, Mom.' It wasn't an appeal, but rather the verbal expression of a weariness so complete it extended beyond my body, beyond my physical and mental existence; an exhaustion embedded in time itself. 'Let's not fight today. If Marcela offers again, you'll take this money and you'll buy what you need. Okay?'

She rejected the money. She lifted the bills from the table, folded them in half, and held them out to me without even looking my way.

'I'm not leaving you alone in all this,' she said.

'I'm already alone in all this.'

She clicked her tongue.

'You don't know what you're saying.'

I leaned toward her and whispered again that I needed to go. I told her that soon, really soon, the two of us would be leaving for Brazil. I'm almost there, okay? I took the money from her limp hand and set it back on the table. Gravity was pulling me downward: my head, my lungs, everything was being flattened, on the verge of sinking to the depths. I rested my hands on her shoulders, but she resisted my embrace. She was being defensive; stiff and distant, she let herself be pulled backward by the weight of her indignation. I hugged her anyway, and as I did I wondered what I'd been looking for in her all those years. In the end, she and Max were so alike. Nearly my whole life spent waiting, begging . . . for what? It's not even that they refused to give me something; they simply didn't have it to give, and I stubbornly kept fumbling around in an empty well.

'Do you want to help me, Mom?' I said, pressing my lips to her forehead. It wasn't exactly a kiss, more like the sensation of her cold, oily skin against mine. 'If you want to help me, don't make me take care of you, too.'

The old man had fallen asleep in his car with the seat reclined, and he gave a start when I opened the passenger-side door. His body was in such bad shape that he needed to sleep for two minutes for each minute he spent awake.

'Look,' he said, pointing ahead, 'the fog is lifting.'

'Impossible. The alarm didn't sound.'

'Stranger things have happened, and the radio's out.'

Every word seemed to take an oversize piece of him with it, leaving him deflated and coughing. The old man reached over to turn the dial on the radio, but all we heard was the crackle of static. I rolled the window down and stuck my arm out. The temperature hadn't gone up, but there was a new smell in the air, violent and acrid. I could see a fine, greasy substance stuck to the windshield.

'Was this here before?' I asked. The part of my finger I'd run across the glass was all black. 'Dry rain.'

'Soot,' he said. 'Something's burning.'

He started the engine. I looked back at the house and thought I saw my mother in the window, her frame a dark shadow. She made no gesture, and neither did I. That was the last time I saw her. The old man drove off. The streets of Los Pozos were deserted; thinking of the people shut away in their houses reminded me of his canaries singing at dawn.

A little while later a fire truck sped past in the opposite direction with its siren off, followed by two patrol vehicles that didn't even flash their lights at us.

'They're certainly in a rush,' I said.

'There's a *told-you-so* burning their britches,' the old man chuckled as he sped up a little more. 'But seriously, something big is on fire.'

We thought the alarm would sound at any moment, but when we parked in front of Clinics, people were still out in the street like normal. The old man looked up at the building's windows. It was like a giant honeycomb—whoever entered ran the risk of getting trapped forever in its sticky liquid. I handed the old man his four hundred pesos; he slid one of the bills under the seat and the other into his shirt pocket.

'Better safe . . .' he said.

Three or four people had gathered nearby, getting ready to fight over the cab.

'What's your daughter's name?'

'Adelina. I'm Victor Gómez. Nice to meet you.'

He reached out his cold, bony hand, and I shook it.

'Nice to meet you.'

The old man gave me one last look and then peered through the dirty windshield at the passengers waiting their turn.

'Look at that, kid. You brought me luck.'

Do you remember that day?

Which day?

That day. I watched you through the window as you left.

Liar.

You walked like you were on a balance beam.

Balance was never my forte.

Was it because of that woman?

You met her?

Yes.

What was she like?

She had the neck of a bird.

It took me over half an hour to reach the front desk. The receptionist had an identification card hanging from her jacket pocket. In the photo she was smiling, but in person her nose and mouth were hidden behind a blue surgical mask. The women who worked these government jobs had been transformed into strange odalisques of the State by their face masks. She watched me, her eyelashes artificially curled above the blue line that divided her face, while I spelled out Max's name.

'They're not letting anyone in,' said the man after me in line. 'Ask anyone. This is the third time I've lined up today.'

'He's in chronic care,' I said.

There was something in those words that immediately softened the disposition of any bureaucrat, and the odalisque typed away on her keyboard. Then she spun around in her ergonomic chair and her quick nails flicked through her card box until she landed on mine.

'Second elevator, tenth floor,' she said, handing it to me.

The line immediately swelled with a groan, moving like a boa constrictor, and spat me out to the side.

'Wait,' I said. 'I want to see someone else. Miss Adelina Gómez.'

The man behind me, who had already moved up, stepped back

into line with an angry snort. His face was freckled and distraught, his double chin as soft as Mauro's. I heard him talking with the others, heard him say: I got here at nine in the morning, and they couldn't find my card. The odalisque exaggerated the clacking of her acrylic nails on the keyboard and kept her eyes glued to the screen.

I want to pause here; I want to get as close to this moment as I can. Why? Because right then everything was still in its place. A precarious place, yes, undesirable and insufficient, but I had gotten used to the way things were. I'd learned to tolerate it. Like that game with the tower of wooden blocks: you remove one block and then another, starting with the least risky ones and getting more daring until the tower falls. If I could get really close to this moment, I'd be able to see a hand reaching for the wrong piece, to feel the tower shake. Except that there's always a wrong piece. I would never see my mother again, and before long I would never see Max again, either: both would disappear from the timeline of my life, but I want to pause in this moment of grace, of innocence, because none of that had happened yet. The time before doesn't seem so bad to me now; it was simply caught in a way of things, in a *certain* way of things. But then everything was set in motion.

'Adelina Gómez is not a patient here,' said the odalisque with a mechanical chill to her voice, sliding her eyes to the freckled man behind me. I turned to look at him, I'm not sure why, stupefied by what I'd just heard. The murmuring stopped and that might have been when the tower wobbled in its clumsy dance, its dangerous swaying. But it didn't fall, not yet. My mother was in her house and had everything she needed. In a few minutes, I would go upstairs to the chronic care wing and I would visit Max. Mauro was waiting for me in my apartment, sucking on strawberry candies. Everything was under control. I'd had a brush with tragedy, but it was only a warning.

'It can't be,' I said.

The freckled man held his breath, intent on my reaction.

The odalisque looked back at me, her eyes dead under countless layers of makeup. She seemed worn out by so much untransferable emotion.

'You can call the search department, ma'am, if you like,' she said, handing me a piece of paper with the number.

This time I will be pushed from the line completely as I think about the taxi driver and the missing teeth that showed when he smiled; when I finally look up, the freckled man will also be gone.

The serpent molts and is remade, yet it remains the same animal.

I took the elevator upstairs. It was empty for the first time in a year. The man had been right, they weren't letting anyone in, but I preferred not to ask questions. I didn't want to get involved, didn't want to think about anything other than myself; I wanted to rest for a while inside my privilege. I got out at chronic care and greeted the usual receptionist. She completed her protocol and handed my card back to me. Everything was familiar: the highly polished hallway, the murmur of the radio, the door to 1024 left ajar.

'Look who's here!' said Max when he saw me. 'Come in, come in. Patricio and I are in the middle of an important debate.'

In the second bed, the one in the middle, slept one of the chronics. In the bed closest to the wall, a bald man with a thick gray moustache smiled, propped up by three or four pillows. He looked thin and weak, but he no longer had that IV drip—or, apparently, the desire to die.

'Come over here,' Max insisted, 'we need your opinion. Your expert opinion. What do you think is more valuable: life or liberty?'

The smell of tobacco hung in the air, but I didn't see an ashtray or any trace of a cigarette anywhere. I took off my coat and draped it on the back of the visitor's armchair.

'You're not going to give your ex-husband a kiss?'

I walked over to his bed and kissed him on the cheek. His skin was dry and tan, not yellow like the last few times, and his new beard was at its roughest, most painful length.

'You look good,' I said.

'It's the lamps.'

'The lamps?'

'They're bathing us in ultraviolet light, isn't that right, Patricio?' The man nodded. 'We take a little spin around the Caribbean and come back. We're living in the lap of luxury here.'

'It's an experiment,' said Patricio. His voice was gravelly, too deep and booming for his emaciated thorax; a bellow emanating from a rag doll.

'Do you know how long Patricio's been married?'

'Forty-three years,' the man rushed to say. 'Never spent a single night apart until they brought me here.'

'He's taking a little conjugal vacation,' said Max. 'In the Caribbean of Lamps. What do you think?'

'They seem to be working,' I said.

'And so here we are, debating what's more important, life or liberty . . . We have a problem, though, because Patricio keeps saying liberty. Right? But that's no way to do it, that's no way to be a national hero.'

'Isn't that exactly what national heroes do?' I asked. 'Sacrifice their life for liberty?'

'Exactly,' said Max. 'But in this case, if you want to win the medal you have to sacrifice your liberty for life.'

'You see?' Patricio interjected. 'You have a sensible woman there.'

Max let out an exaggerated laugh.

'You're right about that. This one's so sensible she's deadly. And believe me when I say it, I've known her since I was five.'

'Since you were six. You were six when you first came to San Felipe. I was five.'

'But you were mature for your age. So. You would pick liberty, too?'

'I didn't say that.'

'Which is it, then?'

'I don't know, Max. I'm not in the mood.'

'What's the matter?'

'Nothing.'

'You need a light bath.'

I wanted to avoid talking to him about things he couldn't understand, about the exhaustion, for example, and that center of gravity pulling me downward from somewhere deep inside myself . . . My stomach? My feet? He would have just tossed something back at me about how gravity didn't work like that, or else he would have asked me which would be more tired: a bird that had flown a thousand kilometers or an ant that had carried fifty times its weight. Another maze I'd never find my way out of unscathed.

'It's the weather,' I said. 'A phenomenon.'

'We know. We get all the news in here, don't we, Patricio? The nurses don't come around much anymore. They're too busy over in critical care. But we keep ourselves entertained, don't we? We choose life over liberty, because life, in here, is a thrilling adventure. Every day brings a new surprise. And luckily my friend Patricio, my brother-in-arms, finally came to his senses.'

'Not like there's anywhere to go,' said Patricio with his incongruous voice and a shrug of his shoulders.

'I see you've been giving him lessons,' I said.

'But he's right. Think about it.'

I looked at my watch; the time for my visit was almost up, and I thought it strange that the nurse hadn't come in yet to give us our warning.

'Don't worry, they're too busy,' said Max. 'They don't even notice. I feel abandoned.'

'Mauro's home alone,' I said.

'I feel doubly abandoned.'

'Do you need anything? Any money?'

'No, do you?'

'Do I what?'

'Do you need me to need something?'

'Don't start, Max.'

'If I ever get out of here, I'm going to be rich. Who'd have thought it?'

'What are you talking about?'

'The bonus,' interjected Patricio. 'The State's paying out a bonus to patients in chronic care.'

'It has been decreed,' said Max.

Now I understood why the old man suddenly felt life was worth more than liberty: he thought he was going to make it out of the swamp, not just alive, but rich.

'Aren't you happy for us? You always said I had no talent for life, but look at me now.' Seated in his bed, he stretched his arms wide. 'A wealthy man with a remarkable talent for not dying.'

Patricio burst into laughter. Max was obviously euphoric, as I'd seen him so many times before, putting on an act for the world (in this case, for Patricio, but why? Why would he want to put on an act for that pitiful skeleton?) and squeezing every last drop from his expansive personality before plummeting to earth. Because there was only one way down from that kind of peak: not the gracious exit of the humble artist, but a momentous withdrawal, like a diver jumping from the summit of his ego into the abyss of self-loathing.

'But don't worry,' said Max. 'You know I'm never getting out of here.'

'Don't say things like that,' I said. 'Don't talk like that.'

'You're a sensible woman. Get out while you can, doll.'

'That's it. Listen to Patricio. Why don't you leave?'

'My mother asks me the same thing.'

'See that, Patricio? Patricio! Sooner or later we were bound to discover that my darling mother-in-law and I had something in common.'

'You have *me* in common.'

'A harsh reality indeed. But seriously, why don't you go? They need copywriters out there, people who can wrangle phrases and keep us all civilized.'

'Enough, Max. You're out of control. What do the doctors say? How much longer are they planning to keep you here?'

'Why do you want to know? If I leave here, we'll probably never see each other again. Come over here, drop all this . . . Come here and talk to me a little.'

'What do you want me to talk about?'

'I don't know, anything. Tell me something I don't know about you. Talk to me a little.'

'I'm always talking to you. Maybe I should shut up a while.'

'Ah, but my antenna doesn't pick it up. And all I have is this measly antenna.'

I walked over to the window. It wasn't cold, but I could feel the hairs on my arms standing up. I put my coat back on and sank my hands into its still-warm pockets. I'd been in there too long and they hadn't thrown me out. That was new, unlike this manic version of Max I'd known and feared my whole life.

'Did you see this?' I asked.

'Which part? It's a lovely view of Paris, but one gets accustomed to it. Very picturesque and all, but its beauty is pretentious, the beauty of . . . what's the word . . . of respectable ladies in fox stoles. I'm always forgetting that the Seine runs right below us. Did you hear? They say it's contaminated.'

'Look at the soot, Max. Something's burning.'

The sky had changed color; the clouds were black, stormy.

'It's the color of liberté. And that's exactly what I was getting at: who would want to go out into that? Right, Patricio? We've come to our senses. Liberté is too risky.'

Max's voice had become a hum in the background. I saw it clearly as I turned back toward him—white noise that entertained Patricio and lulled the other man to sleep.

'Why are you looking at me like that?'

'Did you know a woman in here named Adelina? Last name Gómez.'

'She a friend of yours? If so, never met her.' He laughed.

'Think, Max. Does the name ring a bell?'

Max turned to Patricio.

'You know lots of women, Patricio. Does the name Adelina Gómez ring a bell?'

'Adelina . . . Adelina . . .'

'I'll be right back,' I said.

'Where are you going?'

'I'll be right back,' I repeated, and hurried out of the room.

I shot past the chronic care reception desk and raced down two or three flights of stairs before a security guard made me get on an elevator. The ground floor was teeming with people. The line in front of the odalisque extended across the lobby and out the front door. I didn't return my card to Forms and Documents, I just left—shaking, determined to stretch the elastic to its breaking point, knowing the pain it would cause when it snapped. I walked as fast as my legs would carry me; when I reached the Obelisk, I was still holding the card with Max's name stamped on the top line.

The sky near the port shimmered with a strange light, like the glow of a distant city. If something was burning, it must have been something big. Big enough to be seen from here. As big as an entire neighborhood. But what? People pointed at the glow, above which a dark cloud of ash was swelling. In the distance, the sirens on the fire trucks sounded like a subterranean whistle. I thought I saw the old man's car on every corner. They all looked like his because they were all coated in the same layer of soot that carpeted the sidewalk. Not a single private cab pulled over, so everyone was doing their best to walk through the slippery paste of ash. It was unlikely, even absurd, but I was afraid of running into the old man, of his recognizing me and offering me a lift. I was afraid of looking him in the eye. A few opportunists had rushed out to sell face masks. The only way to get home was on foot, and even though we were all walking quickly, praying that the alarm wouldn't sound, there was something moving about seeing the streets alive again, filled with people.

I crossed the avenue to walk past the monument to José Luis Amadeo, a bronze sculpture set on a concrete pedestal shaped like a boulder rising from the sea. The bust's head was twice as big as normal, and his shoulders emerged from the rock as if it had swallowed the rest of his body, leaving him without legs to paddle or arms to slice through the water. I stopped in front of it. I studied the figure's nose and overly sunken eyes; I studied his brow, too broad; his mouth, twisted into an unpleasant expression, not solemn but pained, an expression that seemed to say: I gave my life for the nation and look what you've done to it. I studied his hairline, his cheekbones chiseled with fury to make him look more virile, or maybe more like an adult and less like the youth he was when they lifted him out of the river. I stared at the figure, at the bronze symbols that formed something like a ring of laurels around the exaggerated muscles of his shoulders—fish, wet suit, and fins—and nowhere at all did I see the José Luis who had been my friend, the youngest diver in San Felipe, with his seaweed fritters and his superstitions, with his little face and his stifled laugh turned inward like a hiccup. There were flowers on the ground—a few wreaths, but mostly single stems left in every available crack. The bust was already covered with ash, but I didn't bother to wipe it clean; the red wind would blow the soot away that night or the next. Along with the flowers.

The police were everywhere downtown. Some loitered under the awnings of the vacant storefronts; others sat in the patrol vans parked on the corners. And all around them, bags of trash and the smell of trash, but also of burning tires. The medical transport taxis drove slowly, skidding in the mire; the private cars, also occupied, did the same. No one stopped. People skated nervously across the damp ash, their hands and heads buried in their coats. Some of them waved at the police. I kept a wide berth; I didn't look at them or offer obsequious greetings or nods. I felt as if Max could see me from his window, as if he could identify me like a beacon among all those colorful coats.

A woman had climbed onto one of the benches in the Plaza de las Palomas, an austere space without trees or fountains, where the elderly used to sit and throw breadcrumbs to the pigeons. What was she doing? Her boots were caked with grime, and she wore a knee-length checked skirt with an old, shapeless woolen sweater; the layers of clothing she had on underneath it made her look thicker. The woman didn't move; her arms hung limp at her sides. She was like some kind of living statue. Maybe that's how I had looked in the elevator at Clinics. Not so different from that woman, because it was clear that she was full of rage, too, and had done her best to choose between momentum and paralysis. From a distance, I saw a police officer cross the plaza. He was headed for the woman. I moved away, walking backward until I reached the window of an abandoned store, then turned and pretended to study the clothing on the mannequins offering me their strange pose: palms turned upward, fingers spread. In the reflection, I watched the policeman stop in front of the woman. He didn't get up on the bench; he stood there looking at her, his head tilted back. He was saying something to her through his German respirator mask. Then he tugged on her dead arm, which hung there aimlessly. Meanwhile, another police officer had arrived; this one did climb onto the bench, and he took the woman by the shoulders. I thought she was going to scream, that she was going to explode with all the rage stiffening her body, but she didn't resist. She let them help her down and walk her to the patrol van. The three of them passed close enough to me that for a few seconds I could hear the officers talking about something. What? Maybe the fire. They mobilized all units, said one, his hands firm on the woman's arms.

I fixed my gaze on the mannequins through the grime covering the window: splatters, fingerprints, remnants of words traced in the dust. The owners of the store hadn't bothered to clear anything out. Clothing still hung on the back wall, summer outfits: a white sundress, espadrilles, wide-brimmed hats with colorful bands. All of it obsolete—not out of style, because nothing had come to replace it, but ridiculous, anachronistic. Like a museum of the absurd. The heads of the other two mannequins were bare and gleamed white over their featureless faces, caught forever in an impossible summer.

They say that thought is tied to the body's movement. That mental processes are sparked by repetitive actions, as if the brain slipped into a state of hypnosis and released the ideas that had been lodged inside. Actions like walking, they say, like washing the dishes. I don't know how true any of that is; I don't know if movement could actually work like a snake charmer for ossified connections. What I do know is that by the time I'd reached the plaza with the bust of José Luis, which had officially been renamed after my friend, the first dead diver, I realized that the old cab driver had reminded me of don Omar. Not the one from before, but the one I saw recently, twenty-seven years after Delfa died. They were similarly gaunt, their chests puffed out like rickety wooden crates; they also talked alike.

When I finally tracked him down, don Omar was no longer the hardy man who could lift a side of beef down from the hooks from which it hung open like a tent and transport it on a wheelbarrow to the piecing table. He'd lost the appetite that came with physical labor, the way he used to scrape the last morsels from the plastic containers Delfa would bring him. He'd become an old man with a head as pink as a newborn rodent, more hair in his ears than on his head, and a loose set of dentures that were too big for his emaciated body. It had been twenty-seven years since the last time the three of us sat in the old factory's break room, him with his stained coveralls and his darkened fingernails that smelled of dried blood. I'd gotten his address by going door-to-door on the hill until I found a man who knew him; they'd worked together on the piecing floor. Don Omar lived with his son and his younger sister, the only one left alive, who was also a widow.

'Delfa never told me she had a son.'

I was surprised.

'It's just that the boy never was quite right,' said don Omar. 'At fourteen he slammed the front door and he was gone for good. We knew. We knew he was running around, doing things he didn't learn under our roof. People are born the way they are, you can bet your life. He didn't even come to the funeral. What do you think about that?'

'I didn't go, either.'

'He was a grown man. The whole neighborhood came to say goodbye to Delfa, except him. A little while later, the bullet he'd been dodging finally caught up with him. Goes right into his skull, but he finds a way around all that death he has inside him and holds on, laid out like an animal but still breathing. A far cry to say he's alive, though, kid. Poor thing can walk and tend to his needs, and he doesn't bother anybody, but he'll never say another word. The bullet soothed his soul and broke his mind. But look at you . . .'

'Delfa never mentioned a son,' was the only thing I managed to say. I suddenly felt as if I didn't know her, and it terrified me.

We also talked about the old meat-processing plant. Don Omar had retired years before they closed it, so the change didn't affect him personally.

'Was the factory old? Sure, it was old. But not everything old has to be thrown in the trash. The place produced well and observed safety protocols. They didn't shut it down because of health concerns. It was something else.'

'Like what?'

'Couldn't tell you, kid.'

'Are you sad that they shut it down?'

'I'm sad that I'm old and don't recognize anything around me. It's a different world.'

'I don't recognize anything, either, don Omar.'

'But the world still recognizes you.'

'You're not frightened by what's going on?'

'Don't worry, kid. None of that's going to kill me. I'll die when I choose to.'

A week later, I went to visit him again. This time his sister, a robust woman, opened the door for me. She showed me to the room where don Omar had his small, unvarnished pine bed; before we entered, she told me he was asleep. We stood for a while in the doorway watching him lie there, rigid.

'He's been like this since your last visit,' his sister said. 'He refuses to eat. He just sleeps and sleeps, and when he does wake up, he's disoriented. He looks around and when he recognizes me he falls into a terrible mood, grumbles, and goes back to sleep.'

We moved closer. His breath was a thread, his chest barely rising and falling.

'Don Omar,' I whispered. 'Don Omar, it's me.' But he didn't want to wake up. He was sick and tired of this life, its attachments.

He died two days later. At the funeral, I saw a man who must have been around fifty years old in flip-flops with white socks and a checked shirt hanging over his pants. The stringy hair covering his eyes gave him a childish appearance, but his beard was white and his shoulders hunched. He showed no emotion, and his eyes were half-shut the whole time, like he was struggling to stay awake.

It would be like a museum.

What kind of museum?

A museum of lost things.

And what would be in it?

Beach umbrellas and those sets with sand pails and shovels
    that come wrapped in netting.

The rake.

The starfish molds.

Some things can't be put on display.

The smell of Hawaiian Tropic.

The white hairs on your arms, stiff with salt.

What would the worst thing be?

Horsefly bites.

That's not the worst.

The smell of dead seals.

And the best?

I can't remember the last time I saw her. What she said to me before she left, what games we played that day. Was she wearing her wig? She must have been. But I don't remember. I tried for years, with the naive zeal of a person who believes that life is linear, that memory is a straight, neat line drawn between two points. But have you ever tried to draw a straight line without a ruler? You'll spend years trying to steady your hand, making the same failed movement over and over; memory is those ant tracks on the page. Delfa used to call Max a brat. The summer she came with us to the beach, she called him a know-it-all brat and swiped at his rear with her broom. But she also hugged him, squeezing his bony, narrow shoulders and kissing the top of his head. You two are going to give me ulcers, she said. But Max's memory of Delfa was colorless, mute; he didn't even remember her wig. You don't remember when she got knocked over by that wave? No. You don't remember her croquetas?

But you were there.

Memory is a broken urn: a thousand shards and fragments of dried mud. What parts of you remain intact? You slip in the mud, lose your balance. And it had been such a delicate balance, one you'd tried so hard to keep, only to fall flat on your ass.

Hahaha, look at you.

There is no graceful way to fall.

I left without saying goodbye to Max. I left, skating across the ash. It was done, but I was still doing it in my memory, over and over, and right now I'm on the verge of doing it again, and I will, despite everything, despite myself. If I can see the future, it's only because I can't stop repeating it. I will leave Clinics again with my blue card in my hand, convinced I'm distancing myself from Max once and for all (wanting to believe it, as if distance were simply a question of putting one foot in front of the other).

My straight line gets tangled; I feel my pen stroke waver and my drawing is suddenly a rope I'm tying around my own neck. Past, present, and future pass through the grinder of memory and fall mingled into a sterile vat. Individual recollections are sprayed with ammonia to force their agglutination, to give them texture. When was the last time I saw Delfa? Not long ago, in dreams. But in reality, when was it? She had her wig, she was sick, but she still came to the house. We still walked to the old processing plant at noon with those plastic containers in a bag, and don Omar had still had us shown into the aquamarine break room. She was thinner, but I don't remember that. Don Omar told me a long time later, and I adopted it as a memory of my own. She looked gaunt, feeble—or sickly, as he put it, because not even the words to describe her are mine. She probably gave me a sickly kiss. Maybe I didn't even look up from the game absorbing my attention. Bye now, sweetheart, she must have said to me, like she always did. And then she won't return the next day. Or the one after that. My mother will take me to the office with her, she has no one to leave me with. Who told her? It didn't seem like it was planned. It must have been over the phone, but who called? Delfa? Don Omar? And who picked up the phone? It could have been me. My mother never got off the couch when she was home, she would just say: Go on, pick it up. I picked up, and it was Delfa's voice on the line. She called me sweetheart. She said, put your mom on the phone, I need to talk to her about something important. And I said: Are you coming today? No, I didn't say that. I didn't say anything. Delfa didn't call; it was don Omar who told my mother that Delfa didn't have much time left, and my mother didn't know what to do, so she took me to the office with her and I spent the whole day drawing at her desk.

When I asked my mother if Delfa would be back the next day, she said no. Delfa is sick, she said, she needs a vacation, she can't be taking care of you all day long. My mother sometimes took a vacation from family life, too; she disappeared for the weekend and always came back looking rested, young, with her hair straightened and her face glowing. I aged her, I ruined her skin like someone pawing the first page of a new notebook until it discolors. I imagined a similar thing would happen to Delfa, that she'd return from her vacation with her bottle-blond hair, which was thin and oily but at least didn't smell like mothballs; with her fake teeth, which had brightly colored gums and a metal wire on both sides where they attached to the few real teeth she had left. She would return without a trace of her illness, and my mother would give her a pot of Nivea cream for her cracked hands and her elbows, so dry they were white. But Delfa never returned, and then I wasn't allowed to go to the funeral. I didn't speak to my mother for days, but I didn't cry, either. I know my mother once yelled at me: I don't want my daughter seeing that. But I don't remember why she said it, what I'd asked her, what

I'd pushed for. Did my mother treat Delfa well? She gave her hand-me-downs and paid her a Christmas bonus. Once, she scolded me for hanging off her all day. I don't think she meant it literally. I never touched Delfa in front of my mother, but things changed as soon as she closed the front door behind her. The way Delfa talked to me, the way I talked to her. I gave her kisses on her hands and those same big hands brushed my hair; their weight on my head anchored me in the present. Our corporality was our secret.

It was Delfa who brought home the rabbit. My mother didn't know what to get me for my birthday and asked her: What would she like? I was at that age when toys seemed ridiculous, but I wasn't interested in clothing, either. What would she like? Use your brain, I heard Delfa say in the kitchen, good grief. It wasn't the first time I'd heard her talk about my mother that way. Sometimes she'd roll her eyes and say: God grant me patience. What would she like? A pet, a little animal. Delfa arrived with a box one day and gave it to my mother. Later I understood that the box had my rabbit inside, but my mother had traded it for a nicer box with a pretty pink ribbon, and without air holes or chewed-up bits of carrot. The rabbit hopped around our house, nibbling the legs of our furniture, until it was exiled to the balcony. It only came inside at night to sleep in that nice box that was gradually becoming a ratty bed of damp, foul-smelling cardboard. Delfa was tired of sweeping up all those little pellets of crap, but she'd say: Animals ask a lot of you, but they also give. She wouldn't live to see the sky empty of birds. The rabbit wouldn't live much longer, either. One day, Delfa swung the balcony door open hard, as hard as she once scrubbed the veins of my arm, thinking they were ink stains. The door slammed against the wall; by the time she realized the rabbit was there, it was too late. The rabbit didn't die right away. It didn't bleed, either, so we thought it wasn't hurt too badly. It just curled up, motionless, its ears twitching in quick spasms; it wouldn't eat anything. I spent the whole afternoon watching it through the window until Delfa told me to get away from there. It wasn't until my mother got home that we opened the door to find the rabbit stretched out and immobile on the edge of the balcony, its head hanging over the void.

We're in the living room of that old apartment. I recognize the crooked painting on the wall. I recognize the chairs with the broken crossbars, the Paraguayan lace tablecloth. Delfa removes her wig and sets it on the lamp. My mother has just said something cruel to her, but I can't see her reaction, she's facing away from me. I'm curled up on the sofa. Neither of them sees me. Why don't you try taking care of your little girl? Delfa says, and walks toward the front door without a hair on her head. Why does she leave her wig? I want to call to her, I want to get up off the couch and run to her, but I can't. I'm a statue. The living room is darker now because the wig blocks the light that should be coming from the lamp, which suddenly looks like the head of a slender woman. I'm crying, but I think: If she leaves her wig, it's because she's coming back.

If you're given a box full of air, what is the gift?

I left the plazas behind me like distance markers along the avenue, and little by little the streets emptied out. Every so often a figure would shimmer like a mirage in the artificial whiteness, and in that last stretch that led to the port my mood began to shift. I wasn't sure of anything anymore, and might have liked to retrace my steps through the ash all the way back to Clinics. My legs felt heavy; a hot tingling pooled in my calves. The smoke from the fire seemed to get closer as I approached the port, a thick funnel that fused with the clouds. It was coming from the hill.

I stopped to rest near a shopping arcade where there had once been a post office, back when I was a teenager. I'd go there to send Max long letters full of details about my inner world and his responses would arrive in my mother's mailbox, which was just a slot in the wall. I read those letters over and over until I'd committed them to memory. Sometimes I didn't know if a conversation with Max had really happened, or if I'd responded to him in my mind as part of our endless dialogue. I had liked going to that sinister place because it made me feel as if Max and I belonged to a separate realm, insulated against the ugliness and squalor that surrounded us. That was a high point. I still possessed an inner world and still believed that describing it had value. I peered inside; the passageway that had once been lit with fluorescent bulbs was now a dark, fetid throat, a vast junkyard of metal bars and broken glass. I might have thought about going in anyway to see if there was something left back there: scraps, traces, physical proof that those other days once existed. But I didn't and, a moment later, the patrol van appeared.

'Where are you headed?' the officer asked.

'To the port,' I replied. 'Where's the fire?'

'I couldn't say, Miss.'

'But it's big,' I said, pointing at the column of smoke. 'It's coming from the hill.'

'It's nothing serious,' he replied, without turning his head. 'Do you want a lift?'

But I didn't want that, no. I was afraid the world would come crashing down around me if I stopped moving, and when I say 'the world' what I mean is the past, because the fragile and wavering present I'd had until a few hours ago was coming to an end. The patrol van drove away, and I lingered for a few minutes more, leaning against the window of another shuttered store. That was when I tried to match my foot to the print I'd left in the ash. The mark was pristine, you could even see the patterns of my rubber sole. I set my right foot in the right print, carefully, trying to line it up exactly with the ash borders on the paving stone, but it was impossible: the print was always just a little bit bigger, as if my foot had shrunk. And that ridiculous detail, the feeling of a thing that didn't fit and could never fit again, kept me from going back to Clinics, to Max, to everything that extended beyond him.

The last stretch was grueling. There were no medical transport taxis in sight, and the ash was accumulating into a lunar landscape draped in a gauzy halo of fog. There was no turning back, but I couldn't go on, either. That's just a figure of speech, of course; so many things are. Because in the end my legs did their work and I finally saw the greenish-red glow of the Palace Hotel sign, guiding me. I passed under the neon lights, recognizing their electric hum, and walked the last few blocks to my building lobby and its cracked walls, its dead elevator, its paint ballooning out from the humidity. It had taken me hours to get back, much longer than I'd promised Mauro, and I used the last of my strength to climb the stairs two at a time.

When I reached the third floor, I found boxes stacked across the landing. Next to them was an old-fashioned leather suitcase that looked like the round belly of a horse. I could hear someone panting and grunting behind them, then a man stuck his head through the wall of cardboard.

'An angel fallen right from the sky,' he said when he saw me.

His voice was hoarse. He must have been around my mother's age, but judging by the state of his lungs, he'd probably been a smoker all his life. I'd never seen him before, or at least I didn't remember him. Was he a neighbor or a squatter? What difference did it make? I didn't care if he was in there looting, as long as he didn't get in my way. He noticed the hesitation in my eyes, and maybe the annoyance.

'Yeah,' he said. 'I'm leaving, too. Not that I'm ashamed.'

'I didn't know I had any neighbors left.'

'You're the one in 501, right? With the boy?'

The man had a perfect map of the building in his head, and he listed the apartments that were still occupied.

'Not for much longer, though,' he said.

I had to help him with the boxes and the suitcase, which felt like it was loaded with bricks. We carried them down the stairs together and piled them up again in the lobby. The man coughed and wheezed the whole time, mucus purring in his chest. Every so often, he repeated that I was an angel, and immediately struggled to move the phlegm from one lung to the other, unwilling to spit it out in front of me. I avoided asking him how he was going to get those boxes out of there or where he was planning to go; the truth is that I didn't care. I didn't have the strength to invest in him or his boxes, or anything that wasn't Mauro waiting upstairs, alone.

'It's crazy out there,' I said, by way of a warning. 'Something's going on.'

'Something's always going on,' he said. I heard a certain melancholy in his voice, but also a joke made at his own expense. As the man mopped the sweat from his neck with a handkerchief, I wished him luck and started back up the stairs, this time slowly, pressing my palms against one knee, then the other, spurring myself on like a weary mule.

As soon as I opened the door I noticed a strange, sharp odor. I called to Mauro, but he didn't answer. Mauro, I said again, I'm back. A quiet splash was the warning sign. I ripped off my coat and ran toward the bathroom. It was like a battlefield in there. Mauro was naked in the tub, his legs only halfway covered by water, surrounded by containers and containers of food; some of them empty, others full of water. There were shards of glass, metal tops, soggy labels, and scraps of food scattered across the floor. Floating in the bathwater were nibbled pieces of carrot and gherkins—that tart smell was pickling liquid, maybe also urine. Mauro didn't even look at me as I stood in the door, speechless, overwhelmed, processing the mess around him. They were our containers of pickled vegetables, the only kind that reached Valdivia's store from inland, and which I'd had under lock and key in my closet. I counted over ten broken or empty jars, which might have been all we had left. How did he find the key? I went into my room and found all my drawers and closet doors wide open. The floor was a jumble of clothes and soggy papers.

'Mauro, what did you do with the key?' I asked, my muscles shedding their fatigue and tensing with an energy I thought I'd used up. 'Answer me!'

Stuffed and self-satisfied, he will ignore me; he will fill a jar with water and empty it over his knees. He will talk to himself and it will sound like he's singing. My arms and legs will tremble with rage. The broken glass will crunch under my shoes as I walk to the bath-tub and lean over him to grab him by the armpits.

'Get out of there right now. Do you hear me?'

I will strain to lift him, but he will go limp and my hands won't manage to grip his wet skin. I will dig my fingers into the folds of his abdomen and pull like I'm trying to get him out of a wool sweater, but his skin will fold and slide from my hands. He will raise an elbow and I will be brushed off.

'Get up, I said.'

I will try again and his body will rise a few centimeters, but not for long; like a fish, like an amphibious monster, he will slip from my hands and crash against the jars in the tub. The noise will be more alarming than the impact, but it is enough to frighten Mauro, who will start to whine and scream *naaaaa*, *naaaaaa* as he continues to struggle against my efforts to lift him. Water will splash everywhere, and a few jars will roll across the floor. I won't know if I'm hurting him, though I have all ten fingers dug into his abdomen; he will keep shrieking his *naaaaa, naaaaaa,* his skin scratched and red from the struggle, his eyes two long slits in his shapeless face, his nose and lips and brow consumed by his sniffling, his snot, his drool. I will gather my strength and will manage to lift him enough to sit him on the lip of the tub, but in the process I will slip in a puddle and fall on my side with one arm still reaching toward him. My shoulder will hit the bidet. I'll feel an electric jolt, then a hard yank and a wave of nausea as my rib cage hits the tile. I'll stay like that, laid out with my cheek against the wet floor, and as I look up through my tangled hair, I'll see Mauro rise dripping from the bath like a nude statue come to life, like a sinister Poseidon heavy with all the waters of the sea. He will stand, step over me, and walk out. For another moment I won't hear anything, I'll have only the mental image of the puddles he is leaving behind him on the wood floors. Then I will be shaken by the alarm. It will be loud, as if it were coming from inside the apartment, as if our home had no walls, as if we lived on a plywood set filled with cheap furniture. The alarm will pass through the building and through me as if we were both made of tissue. Lying there among the shards of glass, I'll wonder if the windows are shut but won't have the will to get up. Mauro, come here, I will say. Mauro. But he won't come, and I will curl up on the floor and see the eyes of the odalisque before me, her heavy lashes like a curtain of steel.

The cloud of mosquitoes rises from the grass. We slap our legs, hard, and some burst like drops of blood, leave spreading stains on our hands. There is a strong smell. We pass the bar of mosquito repellent around, left to right; we slather even our faces and the backs of our hands. We will suck those fingers later without thinking, swathed in the smell of grilled meat and the *crac crac crac* of the firewood and the crickets chirping slow in the distance. Later, we'll go into the house and smoke will be rising from the repellent coil on a plate on the floor. The ash will fall onto the ceramic like the skin of a snake, dead and gray; the trace of a thing able to consume itself entirely over the course of the night, leaving nothing but a little green tail on its metal base. The next morning, Delfa will run across the sand after a beach umbrella that has been picked up by the wind and is spinning, spinning, spinning. The umbrella keeps going; its pole digs into the sand like a weapon, but not enough to halt its movement. Until someone grabs it. Someone far away, a man, grabs it and waits for Delfa to arrive, gasping for breath, legs tangled in her sarong.

Where are you?

Far away.

Then how can you hear me?

The losses were greater than anticipated. Even with what was left in the kitchen, mostly bags of beans stamped with the red logo of the national processing plant, we'd be out of food before long. Mauro's parents were supposed to arrive the next morning, but they would be delayed by the weather. Two or three days more, I guessed, depending on whether the wind took a turn. Maybe they were already halfway here, waiting in some roadside motel with the weather channel running nonstop on mute. I imagined Mauro's mother sitting on the edge of the bed, knees pressed tightly together, on a scratchy, foul-smelling quilt. No. That wasn't her style, but she might glance at the television in the reception area while sipping a chamomile tea. When the storm passed, she would arrive laden with provisions. Nothing like a good storm to feed one's guilt.

The alarm stopped as I was sweeping up the last of the glass. A few shards had pierced my forearm, and thin streams of blood and water trickled down my wet skin. I cleaned my cuts and put Band-Aids on them. They weren't deep, but they gave me something to think about that wasn't my aching shoulder, which had begun to stiffen, swell, and throb. Without the alarm, you could hear the leaves on the trees in the plaza and the wooden blinds rattling in the early wind. A purplish light had begun tinting the sky, but the smoke from the fire dulled every color. Mauro had fallen asleep. I went to make sure he wasn't still naked, which he was, but I didn't want to wake him, so I covered him with his dinosaur blanket. This could be the last time. All I needed to do was tell Mauro's mother that I was leaving, pack a bag, and ask her for a lift out of the city in her armored SUV. From there it would be easy to get a fake health certificate and cross the border. One last night of wind, one last night with Mauro. But maybe that thought didn't occur to me in the moment; maybe I'm injecting it now into the memory, since it doesn't include my mother or Max. I didn't have the strength to want anything. I went back into the living room and picked up my coat; I found my card from Clinics in the pocket, a slight crease in the heavy paper. I looked at it for a moment. I swear I felt it pulse in my hand like a living thing.

You're trading one child for another, my mother had said when I told her I was leaving Max. The card pulsed in my hand and I couldn't bring myself to tear or cut it up. I smoothed it out with my hand and left it on top of the refrigerator, under a ceramic bowl that had once held fruit. I barely had the energy to go back to the living room, turn on the television, and collapse on the sofa.

I searched for news about the fire. At that hour, channels three and nine only showed old movies; on the national network, an elliptical sun was spinning in the top right corner of the screen like an empanada with hair. They were airing a rerun of one of those documentaries about the new processing plant, this time about the poultry section, marked in yellow on the map. The words HIGH ALERT—STRONG WIND scrolled across the screen below the image of a few featherless chickens dangling from hooks on rails above the women working the line. The gangly, obscene chickens would drop onto the conveyor belt and a line worker would position them, handling them indifferently. She'd been touched that way, too, like a chicken on its way to becoming mechanically separated meat products, a frozen nugget. But at least she had been touched, at least other hands could attest to her existence. The chicken's head hung limp like a flower at the end of a broken stem, but there was no time to adjust its position. The conveyor belt was already bringing another chicken and that body, too, had to be touched with the apathetic skin of rubber gloves. That one, too, will go into the machine; the pressure will separate flesh, tendons, and eyes from delicate bones. Once the soft meat is pulverized, it will pass as a uniform substance through holes in the machine, not unlike a giant colander. This was the real transubstantiation. Inside the machine all chickens are made equal, flesh of their flesh of the same flesh. At the end of her shift, as she drops her gloves and apron and cap and face mask into the disinfection trough, a receptacle for all that has been used and abused, the line worker will think with relief about the bag of nuggets she will take home with her. Back in her street clothes, she will stand in line with the other workers for the boss to look inside her purse and then, at the stamping window, she will be able to buy a bag of nuggets at cost, or maybe even get one for free if there was a quality control issue: they were the same nuggets that ladies would pay two or three times as much for at inland supermarkets—just uglier, just shapeless, just undesirable and discarded. But the same chicken meat, mechanically smashed and combined. The line worker will climb into a private cab with her bag of nuggets and will pay too much for the ride to avoid the red wind; in the car she will think that things aren't so bad after all, that life is still possible. Maybe she will make the driver laugh, or maybe not; maybe better to travel in silence, watching the clouds engulf the street, while in a gabled house that looks like a Swiss chalet with local flowers growing out front, somewhere far away from any toxic river, another woman will open a bag of nuggets and drop them into her new air fryer. Every bit as crunchy, every bit as delicious, but without the unwelcome effects of oil.

I turned the volume on the television down; the wind was so strong I couldn't hear it anyway. The trees seemed about to snap like old hinges. Night had fallen in the middle of the day, its darkness red like congealed blood. Before, when I lived with Max, our window used to look out over a schoolyard. During recess, the children's shouting would distract me from my work: Red light, green light, one, two, threeee! Sometimes I hated them. I didn't know how much worse it was to be alone with the sounds of nature, its profound indifference. I didn't even know the game those children were playing. Red light! Green light! Delfa only came with us once to San Felipe, and that was the summer she got knocked over by a wave. She was standing at the water's edge, watching me as I bodysurfed in the shallows on a foam boogie board. The water didn't reach halfway up her thigh, but the wave lifted her off her feet. We saw her disappear and then reappear on the sand, her hair all tangled and her body stretched out like a dead seal. The adults helped her to her feet. Her bathing suit had shifted, exposing one heavy breast and its large pink nipple. Stupefied, she let herself be helped. Later she told me that everything had gone yellow and murky, and said maybe that's what death looked like: not black but yellow, and that silence like a motor running in the distance. She said: I didn't even have time to feel scared.

She must have been sick by then, but no one knew it. The two of us sat on the wet sand. Her feet were buried in a little hole she'd dug with her heels and she looked from side to side. Colors suddenly seemed more beautiful, she said, more vibrant. The world around her had taken on new life.

Delfa and I played cat's cradle. Her palms facing one another, splayed fingers, twisted knuckles. My mother's fingers, also splayed. Like her toes separated by cotton balls, their nails freshly painted, her heels resting on the coffee table in front of the television. I had to bring her things: that was our game. I had been an accident, which she saw as a stroke of good fortune. She told me that, many times. According to her, it was the only way to know you hadn't been born to make someone else feel better, to compensate for all their bad decisions.

One time, a little while after don Omar took me around the old processing plant and showed me the machines pressing out thick swirls of pink slime, I refused to eat a hot dog my mother had boiled and cut into pieces for me. The pieces were swimming in a pool of mustard, but I still refused to eat them and she forced them into my mouth. She dug her freshly painted fingernails deep into my cheeks and stuck the fork inside. I began to cry. That hurt, I said between sobs. I know it did, she said. Why? I shouted. Why? And she replied: Because I'm your mother.

Then, after the hunger and thirst, after days of solitude, an ant
   passes and you look at it like you've never looked at an ant
   before, and you realize that the ant doesn't suffer.
All that to figure out ants don't suffer?
All that to figure out the one looking isn't me.

Two trees fell in the plaza and the wind howled all night. It was the worst storm we'd had so far; it seemed like it was going to tear down the walls. For a moment, I thought I felt the whole building shake. I imagined the worst, but somehow it seemed all right; I was relieved to think it might all be over soon. I pictured a hole under the rubble, a little cave tucked away from the fog and the sound of the wind, and imagined how peaceful that would be. The phone lines had gone down overnight. The spokesperson for the State made assurances that the technicians were working hard to get them back up. There was no service inland, either. The central tower was located in the city and had been, as they said on the news, seriously damaged by the red wind.

When I tried to air the apartment out that morning, a foul odor rushed in and I had to close the windows right away to control my nausea. I turned on the television and flipped to the ten o'clock news. They were talking about El Príncipe and how many antennas and trees had been knocked down, but no one said anything about the fire or the putrid stench coming from the fog. It wasn't until noon that regular programming was interrupted and the Minister appeared on the national network in front of a swarm of reporters and microphones. He said: *accident, setback, contingency*. Then, as if in a dream, we heard him announce the impossible: a fire at the new meat-processing plant. A murmur went up among the crowd, the flutter of reporters jostling one another like frenzied birds. They flapped recording devices, papers. The fire started at around eleven in the morning the day before, said the Minister. He trotted out his lexicon of inoffensive phrases and technical terms, but without much conviction. We'd all seen the soot and slid through its dark film, we'd all breathed in the toxic smoke, and now we all understood that our flashy new processing plant was nothing but a pile of ashes. That was the source of the nauseating stench: animals and chemicals burned to a crisp, vats charred like old tin pots. The Minister looked defeated, crumpled in his seat like a raisin; he barely lifted his head to look into the camera. He said: No fatalities were recorded. He sounded as vulnerable as a child who had just lost his parents, and it's true that the fire had turned us all into orphans, in a sense. I thought about the animals. No one considered them victims. They had been saved from becoming pink slime, but they hadn't been saved from the fire. As luck would have it.

The fire had been eating away at the steel entrails of the plant for more than twenty-four hours because the storm had interrupted the work of the firemen. There was no way to go out with that much poison in the air. Outside, army helicopters flew over the rambla. Emergency rooms were packed with respiratory ailments. I spent hours in front of the television that day. It was strange to watch panic make everyone's face look the same—eyes bulging against the delicate material of the lids, cheeks hollowed—giving us all something like a family resemblance. What are we going to do?

The question was repeated like a prayer, and reporters struggled to find an expert willing to tell everyone to stay calm and offer the solace of a lie. Each time someone mentioned Clinics, my heart bucked in my chest. Maybe that was the only sign that I was still alive; my desire for Max, stronger than any bacteria, refused to die. They talked about air quality, about evacuating the patients, about how the hospitals inland wouldn't take them. No one mentioned the chronics.

Mauro was still in his room. He wasn't in a time-out; I had understood long ago how useless it was to punish him for what the syndrome did. What would he learn from that? Dominated by genetics, innocent as a rabbit. His impulses were a bottomless pit, a centrifugal force that absorbed everything, including him.

By late afternoon the fog had returned. On television, they were saying that the fire had been contained. I couldn't see the fallen trees in the plaza anymore. It was just a cloud—thick and low, but just a cloud—and thinking about it like that was a comfort. I got off the sofa and went back to Mauro's room. The plate I'd brought him a few hours earlier was on the floor, spotless, as if he'd licked it clean. He was sitting next to the bed, playing with his Legos. He'd put on his favorite shirt, twisted, and a pair of swimming trunks that bit into his hips.

'Is that a boat?' I asked.

He didn't look up. He was trying to attach a yellow piece in the shape of a Z to a red piece.

'Flying castle,' he said after a while.

I approached him, trying to measure his reaction.

'You don't want to put on some socks?'

He said no. He had just finished adding a second yellow wing to his flying castle.

I sat next to him on the floor. I touched one of his feet; it was cold, and he didn't pull away. His bulbous instep looked like a gasping fish out of water.

'Let's take a look at that belly,' I said, leaning over to lift up his shirt a little. He didn't have any bruises, just a faint scratch on his side. I, on the other hand, had an enormous bruise sprawling across my hip like the map of a new country, and my shoulder was a bit swollen. I stayed there, next to him, with my head between my knees. Mauro muttered something.

'You go in here and here you drive and here you leave.'

I looked over at his window, a rectangle with protective grating.

'The fog is back,' I said.

'The castle can fly in fog,' he said.

'And who's the pilot? You?'

His head wobbled as he lifted the castle and made it turn in the air, making sounds like a motor. They should have come to pick him up by now, but the roads were probably still closed.

'Do you know what's above the clouds?'

'Boats,' he said.

'No, not boats. There are stars, lights. And other planets.'

He remained transfixed by his game, cocooned in a space I couldn't enter. Years of life and mistrust separated me from that realm where everything was possible, from those fantasies that made the world a better, kinder place.

'Are you excited to see the horses?' I asked. 'Your mom is on her way here to get you. You'll ride horses and visit the donkeys.'

Mauro didn't react at all; it was as if he didn't hear me, as if he didn't remember life in the countryside. He never mentioned his mother. He never talked about the time we were apart. I wondered what his memories were like, whether he had a sense of the past or if his illness held him captive in an eternal present, a here and now made of hunger and craving. I left him playing and went back to the kitchen. As I passed, I picked up the telephone. The line was still dead.

You're angry.

I am.

Are you angry because you left, or because you want to return?

A team of divers went into the river to investigate why its waters had expelled the fish like a giant stomach. They had orders from the Ministry of Health. They had instruments and maps. They were to take samples of the riverbed, the seaweed, the mystery lurking in the depths. But the stomach expelled the divers, too, coated in its acid. It did this silently. The divers thought everything was fine; they emerged from the water with their little jars and their big smiles and posed for the requisite photo that appeared on all the newscasts. It wasn't until a few days later that the symptoms began, and José Luis Amadeo became a horrific omen of what awaited the others.

There were no miracles for the divers, who were laid to rest with full state honors. They aired the funeral live: three caskets draped with the flag. The cameras focused on the cemetery, its beautiful tombs, the flowers stirring in the stiffening breeze, the serious expressions on the faces of the ministers. Their hair was being blown around and the President's tie refused to lie flat; he needed to secure it with one hand as if he were holding his heart and lungs in place. We'd known a storm was coming since that morning, but we all thought it would hold off until after the funeral. Why did we think that? The families were there. I recognized José Luis's mother in the first row; she hadn't changed much, she just looked shorter and broader, less imposing than the thick arms that used to pass us fritters through a side window. Beside her were other wives, mothers, sisters, and other sons of San Felipe's divers—sons grown into men, grown into divers themselves. We saw their clenched fists, the coffins reflected in their sunglasses, the stripes of the flags. The only eyes visible were the President's: dry. Before the ceremony had ended, the storm broke. There was lightning and wind, but not a drop of rain. The flowers were sucked into the air and the flags began to flap wildly like sheets on a clothesline, baring the glossy wood of the coffins. One of the three held the body of José Luis, my childhood friend, the first diver to go into Clinics and never come out. We saw a man run over to anchor the flags, which were about to come loose, as if the wind wanted to take their souls with it as well; then we saw the President rushed to safety, surrounded by his guards. He and the ministers were escorted into the presidential motorcade and driven away as lightning flashed on the horizon.

The first red wind, a fierce electrical storm, ruined the divers' funeral. The next day, the President called for an evacuation of the coastal region. The heads of state built new houses on the side of some small hill in the low, endless countryside and started giving orders from there. This is how our new official story begins.

When you read a history book, it's easy to forget that someone was there, someone of flesh and blood. In this story, that someone is me. I was there when the fish appeared; I went down to Martínez Beach and saw how they covered the shore like glittering trash, pieces of cans and glass washed up by the tide. I saw children playing down there, walking on that new sand made of flesh, treading carefully, bending over for a better look at the open mouths and dry eyes. The tiny waves would lift and tug at them, giving them the momentary appearance of life, only to drop them back on the sand like so many old bottles. There were fish floating in the water, too; the beach was so full that the waves couldn't get rid of all of them. I saw children playing without face masks or suits, and I saw adults sorting through fish on the shore, looking to fill their buckets with the ones still struggling to breathe. It wasn't until a team from the Ministry arrived that they got the children out of there and cordoned off the area. That's what they aired on the news: the yellow tape surrounding the beach and the crowd on the other side, curious but safe. I saw the President announce the evacuation of the coastal neighborhoods on the emergency broadcast system. The most important thing is to stay calm, he said, the Ministry of Health is working on this. But no one was listening, because they were too busy running around their houses, packing suitcases, unplugging appliances, gathering money and jewels; money in fat rolls stuck between clothes and sweaty skin, bills growing soggy in underwear, bras, and socks; fingers that couldn't hold another ring, wrists a riot of bracelets. By the time the broadcast was over and the national anthem began to play, people were already loading up cars, boarding up windows, taking seascapes down from their walls. They were buckling in their babies and dragging along their elders, even the ones who said they were born there and wanted to die there. Why do we all want to die where we were born? What's the point, if nothing stays the same anyway, if the place will have become unrecognizable by then? They dragged their elders along, even if they had to break their hips in the process, and then the city came to a standstill: all those cars got stuck in the only massive traffic jam in the history of our country. I saw it. I was there. I watched it from the sidewalk, standing there with a bunch of other people who'd come out to witness the spectacle, to be part of something we still didn't understand. How many of those people are still alive? How many ended up in Clinics? It was a spectacle, all right: an upside-down sofa on a truck bed here, a vacuum poking out of a window there; a tricycle tied to a mattress tied to a luggage rack. Faces framed in car windows, the dirty hands of children pressed against rear windshields. Dogs barking, noses poking out above glass. And a symphony of car horns.

The caravan remained stalled like that, moving so slowly it created the illusion of complete stasis. But it was moving. Three days later the streets were empty again; news cameras transmitted silent highways littered with the trash people had thrown from their windows, and the chaos moved on to another place, somewhere I wasn't. Somewhere I'm not. It became a distant story told by others who also said: I was there.

That's how it happened.

Two more weeks had to pass before I accepted that Mauro's parents weren't coming for him. That it wasn't because of the fire, or the roads, or the dead telephone lines. They had abandoned him. Can I say I was surprised? In retrospect, there had been subtle warning signs everywhere. I spent the next few days rationing food and waiting for the poison in the air to thin enough that I could go out to search for an underground market. We ate little; I ate even less than Mauro, who was strangely docile despite his constant hunger and our shrinking portions—despite the dry, monotonous food and the pink slime permanently ground into our palates. All things considered, those were peaceful days. Days when I didn't think about my mother, or Max. Life focused in like a funnel on Mauro, his stomach, his nocturnal whimpers. My exhaustion had begun to feel like an abscess, a pus-filled ache that could only be soothed by slicing. There was no room for anything else. I had no plan B, and part of me imagined that our new life would be exactly the same. Why wouldn't it? Besieged by the algae, sinking in a swamp of fog.

The air toxicity levels were still so high that not even the patrol vans were out. That's what they said on the news. The national network drones flew over the streets, unable to rise above the first ring, transmitting images of desolate neighborhoods, of dirty foam from the river tumbling across the rambla like dustballs. We resigned ourselves to waiting, and the waiting we did somehow seemed a lot like faith. Faith that the fog would return. When? Someday. Until one day, it did.

I asked so little of you.
But you wanted everything.
I asked so little.
But you never allowed me to ask anything of you.

I went out in the afternoon when the fog was at its most dense. I walked the first two blocks slowly, hunting for signs, adapting to the opacity and its stench of fermented garbage. The desolation of the place wasn't defined anymore by the absence of people: all sound had been sucked into a padded box. The fog pressed firm as a muscle against my body, forming a kind of amorphous suit. In the distance behind me, a motor broke the tomb-like silence. It was impossible to ignore, but I pretended not to hear it until a red car with white splotches eating into its paint drove up to me slowly. The connective tissue of fog seemed to resist its movement, but the car pushed its red snout, its splotch of color, forward through the gray. The driver looked at me through the window. He gave me a bad feeling: his face like an undercover cop's, too square and too neat; his thick arms stretching the sleeves of his shirt; his soft hands. No one had enough food to look like that anymore. Word had been spreading among the taxi drivers about cleanup squadrons that rounded up vagabonds and disappeared them. Maybe they took them to Clinics, which was nearly the same thing; either way, those men and women were never seen sleeping on the street again. I quickened my pace and waved a *no* at him. He stayed a few meters back with his headlights on. He'd placed his bet and I held the losing hand. The crunch of his tires on the pavement, like a snake gliding through scrubland, cracked the air. But I knew the neighborhood, its cartography of doorways and dead ends, and I remembered that after the corner there was a building that hadn't been bricked over. I kept walking, playing it as cool as my body would let me, until I reached the front door of the building: two tall panels of faded wood.

I was received by the uninhabited cold inside, where the fog thinned like a trail of smoke arriving from far away. I took a few steps across the trash and rubble and stood there, hidden behind one of the doors, listening to the hum of the motor. Each sound was distinct, sharp and clear like a landscape. I heard the engine cut off and the car door open, then slam shut. For a moment, the silence absorbed the man's footsteps; maybe he was standing there, waiting for a clue. Then I heard them again. They were getting closer. Just when I thought he was about to come inside, the footsteps grew porous and went silent. Holding my breath, I tried to peek through the line of light above the door's hinge, but it was too thin to see anything except a shadow that interrupted the glow for a moment and then vanished again. The man was moving around out there. Had he not seen me enter the building? Now the sound of plastic crinkling and again the muffled footsteps, the trunk swinging open. Plastic. A plastic bag being gripped. A hand closing around a plastic bag and then a thud, like a shovelful of sand. It took me a moment to understand that the man was carrying something, and that the something was bags of garbage. He went back and forth until, I guessed, he'd filled the trunk, because

I heard him slam it shut and then get into the car and start the engine. The tires crackled over the crumbling asphalt and the car drove slowly away.

I waited an absurdly long time, until long after he'd been absorbed by the egg carton that the city had become. I didn't try to guess what was behind the black market for garbage, but I did think how the city was like a vast free trade zone with a volatile, mysterious economy. I couldn't hear anything at all now. The silence was painful. Who could have imagined the sonic emptiness of a city without the buzzing of insects, but also without the slow grumble of elevators or the murmur of radios through the walls, all those artificial things that—I realize now—were what we called life. Just then, I thought I heard footsteps in the building. They seemed to come from upstairs. It could have been an auditory hallucination, an aural mirage, because silence has that effect on the ear, but there at the end of the hallway a half-collapsed staircase twisted upward into the shadows. I skirted around an upturned chair and a few pieces of burned wood. There was ash on the floor from old cooking fires, blackened sticks crumbling into coal. Traces of pillage, the fate of all these abandoned buildings. I climbed the stairs slowly, straining my ears. The silence had returned in all its savagery, and each step I took released a chunk of plaster or shard of glass. What was I looking for? I obviously wasn't going to find an underground market there. The front doors of all the apartments on the first floor had been ripped from their frames. Their interiors: outlets and baseboards and faucets missing, graffiti and broken glass, hinges rusted by the humidity. I pressed on into the heart of the building; no one could possibly live like that, without windows or any other protection against the red wind. When I turned to leave, I sensed a movement in the stairwell, near the second floor.

'Is anyone there?'

Not even an echo.

'I want to buy supplies,' I said. 'Food.'

I approached the stairwell and looked up at the steps covered in rubble and scraps of metal. A nauseating stench rose from the floor. I began to climb anyway, trying not to touch the walls even when I struggled to keep my balance. I felt around with my foot for a stable surface before taking each step. A crimson moss was growing in the empty window frames. Could that be what stank? I pulled my scarf over my nose and immediately felt the damp air of my own breath. The reddish moss was made up of tiny round leaves plump with moisture.

The scene on the second floor wasn't much different: trashed apartments, all except one of which were missing a front door. As I got closer, I saw that what had looked like a door left ajar was in fact a graft that didn't quite fit the frame. I couldn't see anything through the crack, but thought I could make out the rustling of fabric, as if someone had crossed their legs or turned over in their sleep.

'Anyone there?' I asked, pushing the door with my foot.

I kept pushing until I'd made an opening big enough to pass through sideways. I stuck my shoulder in first; when my body was halfway inside the room, its walls sooted by countless fires, I saw the cage. Next to a window with a heavy black garbage bag where the glass would have been, a big white cage with thick bars and fancy ornaments, a bit banged up but still elegant. Inside, an animal—a bird?—motionless, frightened.

'Hello,' I said. 'Nice to meet you.'

I heard the rustling sound again, clearer now. The bird had moved, a slight and monstrous shake of its wings. On the floor, among the rubble: charred pieces of wood and empty plastic bottles, some of them cut to make bowls; a mattress without sheets or blankets, sunken in the middle and torn in places where bits of foam rubber poked through. The stench got worse as I approached the cage. Then I noticed—not far from the mattress, and not far from a small pot black with soot, either—human excrement on the floor. The bird seemed like another hallucination, but when I was finally standing in front of the cage I knew that it was real, that it was dying. It had white growths on its beak and eyes. It couldn't see me because of that festering substance, but it sensed my presence and shifted nervously.

'Who is it that needs you so badly?' I asked, and my own voice terrified me.

The bird shuddered and made that hushed sound again with its dull feathers, which must once have been blue, maybe iridescent and exotic as pearls, but which had gone ashen and barely moved with the tremor that ran through its body, its only sign of life. I unfastened the little wire that held the cage shut and swung back the door. The opening was tall enough for the bird to pass through without bending, but it didn't move. Its wings were clipped, dead. I stood there a moment, looking at it, and immediately rejected the idea of taking the cage with me. My nose had begun to itch and I felt like my throat was burning, like I had that whitish substance clinging to me. Like my eyes would soon be covered over, consumed by the fungus, shut forever to the putrefaction around me, finally,

finally rotting alongside it all, sores in my throat, the skin of my nose eaten away. How many more winds until that bird was free? How many until I was?

I left the cage open and backed away. I hurried down the stairs as fast as I could without stumbling, and the street welcomed me with its monochromatic gleam. The air felt fresh compared to the stench cooking inside. I started off along San Jerónimo. The fog kept pace with me like a loyal dog, though I could only catch partial glimpses of its vast gray flank, pressed always between me and the things around me. I turned again, this time onto Asunción Norte. Not one window open a crack, not one lookout, nothing that could be read as a sign of illicit activity. One door had a white skull painted above it. Others had been forced open. The street was impassable, a tangle of fallen electrical wires, and no other car followed me.

I thought I saw a shape in the distance, a long thin mass puncturing the elastic mesh of the air. Another mirage. It was hard to breathe. The fog had become cement hardening my lungs. I walked a little further, each step a useless movement. There is nothing around and I know there will be nothing. But a few blocks later I will look up at the facade of one of those old colonial homes with iron balconies and see a man's silhouette in the window, his face close to the glass and a glowing ember between his lips. When he senses my gaze, the man will hide behind the curtain. That is when the alarm will sound. The noise will arrive and suddenly it will be everywhere, like they say of intensely white landscapes, of snow or salt, where there's no point of reference, no up or down, no beginning or end.

I will hurry home, feeling the fog already lift, thinned, about to be erased by the wind, and when I open the door Mauro will be curled up in a ball on the sofa with his hands over his ears. I will lie down next to him. He will say nothing, aside from that look of longing, that moment his eyes open just a little bit wider and show his relief. I will hug him, and the air from my down jacket will rush out as if someone were squeezing a pillow.

'Wind,' Mauro will say.

'Yes, love, it's the wind. That's all.'

His skin will be damp, not from sweat but from recent tears collected in the folds of his neck. I will touch my nose to that moisture, then my lips. The tension will leave his body and he will wrap his arms around me; I will feel his fingers in the fake fur trim of my coat. It's like a foxtail and he will stroke the fur, brushing it gently with his eyes closed. Everything's all right, I'll say, I promise. His breathing will begin to slow as my mouth fills with the blood oozing from my gums.

'Hungry,' he will say.

'Guess what. I saw a bird. A beautiful bird with bright feathers.'

'Is it hungry?'

'Yes, but it flew all around the sky. Do you want to hear about it?'

Mauro will rest his head on my shoulder. The hole in his stomach will shrink for a moment. But not for long.

Imagine you told me everything you thought.

Okay.

You'd never stop talking, because as soon as you told me one
    thing, you'd have another thing to say, and then another,
     and another. Can you imagine? You'd never stop.

Sometimes I don't think about anything.

When?

Now.

Not true: you're thinking that you're not thinking about anything.

What do you think about?

I think about birds.

Actually, I think about the days after the first red wind: the panic, the uncertainty. The phone calls from friends reciting contradictory theories, each one clinging to their truth and then justifying their decision to leave: the life worth living, the body worth saving. Their desperate lists of reasons. For what? It's better to live like a rat than to not live at all. It was funny how they thought they needed reasons. How they couldn't accept that our lives were driven by chance, maybe by inertia. And why did they need to tell me? No one had asked them to explain themselves, but they all called, offering motivations, comparing strategies, dusting off old ideas about survival instincts and the preservation of the species. They called so I could validate their decision, so I could encourage their discourse of *life at any cost*. And when they were met with detachment bordering on indifference, they tried to change my mind by showing me the bright side, as if they were out there saving souls. When they failed, they turned vicious so quickly it was clear their animosity had always been there. They blamed me for everything, even their own misfortune.

The worst part came a few weeks after the disrupted funeral for the divers. It had been overcast for days and the temperature had

risen, even though it was the middle of winter. People started talking about a second summer. Every day we waited for rain, repeating
how the dry spell couldn't possibly last, but somehow it did; every
morning we woke up and confirmed that it hadn't rained overnight,
either. We watched the storm gather above us, in a world of black
clouds and whirlwinds, a distant battle of the skies. Meanwhile,
we were being flattened by the unseasonable summer that swelled
our legs and had us gasping in the humidity. The storm arrived a
few nights later, when no one expected it anymore, when everyone
thought it would pass us by. Late that afternoon, the sky began to
fray like a tarpaulin finally giving out, and raindrops burst heavy
against the window that looked out over the schoolyard.

Max had gone out and the house was dark except for the light of
the floor lamp. I raised the blinds so I could watch the rain and sat
on the edge of the sofa, near the phone. I saw my reflection in the
window—hands slack, knees fallen open into a kind of rhombus—
and inside my reflection, or superimposed on it, was the brimming
city: rooftops and buildings of different sizes, but above all antennas, hundreds of antennas and wires. All those antennas, each one
monitoring its own little part of space. Like scarecrows, I thought,
urban scarecrows. I stood and turned off the lamp. The wind shook
the trees; it seemed like it might pull them up from the roots. Every
so often lightning flashed in the distance, silent, and the city seemed
to tremble. I imagined Max hurrying home. He'd left the house that
morning in sandals and a pair of light summer pants that hung
loose from his protruding hip bones. You put too much faith in
this second summer, I had said. The heavens were about to open
over an expectant city; every face was pressed to a window, wait-

ing to behold the miracle. I stood motionless in the dark, focusing on the lights outside the school, which revealed a few horizontal drops. The distant, mute flashes from before were closer now—not as the soft glow that had been illuminating the sky and then fading, but as the sharp outline of lightning, a tree of electricity unleashing its vengeance on us. I counted the seconds between lightning and thunderclap. There it was, getting closer, the triumph of winter. The time between the lightning and thunder got shorter and shorter. Lightning fell on the city, though maybe *fell* isn't the right word, since it was as if the lightning were coming straight from the center of the earth and shattering the pavement on its way up. The city, a terrifying flower, a bud opening to violence with delight. I was frightened. I reached for the phone and dialed my mother's number. It rang several times. It wasn't unusual for her to go out at night; I never asked her where or with whom and she never told me, not because she was ashamed but because she liked to have secrets, to know there was a part of her no one else could access. The phone rang again and again; she clearly wasn't going to answer, but I didn't hang up. I pictured it ringing there in the dark, filling the silence between one thunderclap and the next.

That's how it happened. But the rains never came, and they never would. The next morning we rose, exhausted after a sleepless night, to find ourselves enveloped in fog.

Explain it to me.

Why?

I want to understand.

And what if I say you already know all there is to know?

Then I already know how this story ends.

Nothing is yours until someone else loses or discards it. I knew it then, but not in words, not the way I'm putting it now; the way I knew it was more jumbled, furious. That's it: furious, like the fury of a feeble stalk piercing the seed and forcing its way through root systems and layers of hard earth. What would become of Mauro if something were to happen to me, a brush with the wind or getting scooped up by a patrol van and dropped on the doorstep at Clinics? The idea carved a pit of terror in my body. I traced its jagged edges, exploring them for the first time, full of wonder. I pictured Mauro alone in the apartment. I pictured him opening the windows—doing some unfathomable dance, naked, while the red wind rushed through the empty rooms—or eating until he choked, surrounded by vomit; I pictured him digging around the garbage heap on the corner or wandering along the rambla beside a river dark like bitter wine. I had suddenly lost the right to risk my life. The fear came joined to a feeling of suffocation, the claustrophobia of not being able to leave a cramped space, and that space was me.

We ate chickpeas for dinner again the night I saw the bird. They were bland, doused in oil, tossed with a little pink slime. Mauro didn't complain, but he was hungry again soon after and ate two strawberry popsicles. Later, in the middle of a tantrum, he tried to open the refrigerator and ended up shredding the dinosaur drawings I'd stuck to the door with magnets. He tore them into confetti and stomped on them, then he turned purple from screaming and went hoarse. We'd gone through all our tricks. The syndrome was hungry, and it could kill him if it wanted. Nothing could distract him now: not stories about birds, not our increasingly outlandish and challenging games, not the candies you had to gnaw on like little rocks.

We slept badly. The wooden legs on Mauro's bed creaked each time he tossed and turned; that creaking was with me all night. I got up twice to go to the bathroom. My throat and nose itched, but when I looked in the mirror, under the white light, all I saw were the same wrinkles and spots as always, the same dry lips with thin strips of skin pulled loose by the cold, the fine network of blue veins around my eyes. I went back to bed. In the morning, I gave Mauro my portion of breakfast.

I was just thinking about something Max asked me once: What do you feel when you make a mistake? It must have been shortly before the divorce, or in one of my visits to Clinics, because I remember my guard went up at the question, bracing for the attack. What? I said. When you *make a mistake*. What do you feel? I knew what he felt: anger. I had seen him kick things, slam his fist on the table so hard he knocked over our glasses; I'd seen him literally go blind with rage and, beside himself, slice the skin of his arms then crawl back docile like a wounded dog, seeking my hand, my silence. That was the Max he was trying to annihilate with his gurus and his exercises, with his trips and his visions, but it was also the Max who had loved me, or had needed me, at least. What did I feel when I made a mistake? Not anger but something else, something that turned me fragile and made me feel stupid. It was like hearing my mother's voice asking me to bring her this or that, to fetch the ice tray and place a few cubes carefully in her glass. Don't drip all over the floor, she'd say. The ice cubes would slip from my hands; the metal ice tray would stick to my fingers, and I'd lose skin pulling them free. Shame, I said, but Max shook his head. That's what you feel later, he said; in the moment you're making the mistake, you don't feel anything. It was like Coyote and the Road Runner, he said, when the Coyote runs off the cliff and keeps going, feet spinning full speed in the air. It isn't until he looks down and realizes he's running on air, without solid ground beneath his feet, that he begins to fall.

I guess something like that happened then: I finally realized there was no ground under our feet. If I didn't find food some-where, if they were right after all . . . They, who? All of them. My mother's voice saying: You're the most stubborn person I know. And I'd begun to feel the familiar presence of a deficient being that lived inside me, a black mouth that opened and closed. Sometimes I thought that being and I were one and the same; other times I saw it as a parasite eager to take my place. The black mouth spoke: it told me I was useless, always on the verge of drowning in the tepid broth of my life, that I should let someone else take the wheel. Sometimes I think about those helicopters at amusement parks: the children get in, they pull levers and push buttons while colorful lights blink on the control panel and the helicopter goes up and down. The illusion offered by the ride is so perfect that the children don't realize that their commands aren't moving the helicopter, that someone they can't see is guiding the metal arms that spin them around as they screech in joy and fear.

Is this how things end? An ending is only proof that something else has begun. I refused to see that new beginning, just as I'd refused to see every new beginning, always. I refused to get the money out of my safe and leave the city once and for all; I refused to act on my fake fantasy of rescuing my mother and escaping to Brazil. In my fake fantasy, my mother thanked me: If it weren't for you . . . I heard her say to me, and then to my cousin Cecilia, the schoolteacher, everyone: If it weren't for my daughter . . . It was silly, just a helicopter in an amusement park, because how long would it take the algae to catch up with us there? Even if I could get the health certificates necessary to leave the country, Brazil was joined to the same poisoned sea. So now what? The best way out of a labyrinth is always up, Max used to say. My mother used to say: The labyrinths you build for yourself have no exit.

I tried again, this time with a different route in mind. I was going to walk away from the port and toward the Obelisk, searching the side streets, maybe around the plazas. And if I failed . . . The thought didn't go any further. I headed for the Palace Hotel and passed a bookstore, hermetically sealed behind its metal shutters. The hotel's neon sign flickered at the end of the street. We were buried to our necks in fog, but that greenish-red glow still pulsed like a faint stain, forming a kind of aurora borealis that marked the city's gray body. I walked toward it, drawn in like a moth, passing the old antiques shop. I paused for a moment to look in the window, but all I saw was my own reflection in a coat that made me look like a misshapen doll, like one of those wobbly inflatables kept upright by currents of air. My pockets were stuffed with money, but it wasn't enough to buy even a bag of rice. Who would've thought. The owner of the antiques shop had been an old Italian man who claimed to belong to the aristocracy. Everyone called him the Count. Some said he was a compulsive gambler who'd landed here after fleeing his debts. If that was true, it meant he had experience leaving places in a hurry. I had talked with him a few times; he called me *carina* and once gave me an antique postcard, the kind where people's cheeks and lips are painted red. He would describe himself as an old fox and point to the taxidermied fox he kept on a table. One day I walked past the shop and there was nothing left, not even that moth-eaten creature with its horrifying glass eyes. I pictured the Count's pickup packed tight with books, a Fontainebleau buffet, Henry II furniture upside down on the roof, his seascapes in bubble wrap. Did he predict that seascapes, with their crackling oil paint, would be worth so much one day? It's strange to want to hang on your wall a reminder of what you've lost. I've always been afraid of portraits of dead people, dark oil paintings of one's ancestors. And now I'm terrified of seascapes. The wealthy fought over them at auctions, willing to pay fortunes for a sea painted in colors they would never see again. They fed their nostalgia daily while eating black-market products for breakfast. They bought memories, sure, but it's the lucky ones who can forget.

I kept walking, slowly, peering into every foul nook and cranny of the old buildings along the street, though I'd lost all hope of finding anything around there. The greenish-red stain from the neon sign had spread into an aura, a sphere of color, and I gradually passed into its static hum. The hotel steps looked dirty, and its windows were covered with sheets and blankets. But the place seemed abandoned: the front door, at the top of the blackened marble stair-case, was boarded up by several strips of wood. I was inside the stain now, green and red in their intimate struggle, a shield holding back the fog. From there I watched a car turn near the old corner store. It might have been a medical transport taxi, I wasn't sure. Was it black, or yellow? I hurried to where color met gray and crossed the membrane, sinking back into the world. By the time I reached the cross street, the car had vanished from sight.

The doors of the old corner store had been boarded up for a long time, too, but by now there wasn't a single plank left in place. Some had fallen on their own, rotted by the humidity, and the recent wind had probably just finished tearing down the rest, since the glass was still intact and so were the chain and padlock that held the panels shut. There was no sign of looting. Before the evacuation, the owners had lived in the back and had taken turns to stay open twenty-four hours a day. They even had an ad, a catchy jingle that played on the radio: *We never close, we never close!* On the wall under the shop win-dow, someone had spray-painted: *You're closed now, jerkoff!* I wiped a small circle of the glass clear with my sleeve and tried to see inside. The shelves were empty, except for large bottles of what seemed to be disinfectant or some other cleaning product. Antibacterial soap. Bleach. Mr. Clean. *Kills 99.9% of bacteria.* Steel wool. Polish. Mauro could swallow all that in a second.

I shook the door hard, but the padlock didn't give. Down the street in both directions everything looked dead and desolate under the threatening sky. No sign of the police. I grabbed a loose cobble-stone from the street and swung. The glass shattered. The whole thing came crashing down, but there were still a few sharp pieces trapped around the edges. I plucked them out one by one and tossed them to the ground. When there was no glass left, I stuck my right leg in, but I couldn't bend my torso far enough to fit through where the window had been. I tried again, this time hoisting myself up by the arms and sliding my legs through at the same time, followed by my hips and torso, arching backward and letting my arms slip through last, like the bridges I used to do with the acrobat twins.

Dust had settled onto the long wooden floorboards, and each step I took raised a cloud of lint and grit. The timid light from outside revealed these puffs of congealed time, the residue of countless hours and minutes. I wrapped my scarf around my nose and mouth and tied it tightly behind my neck. I paused at the cash register and pressed a few random keys. It didn't open. They'd cut the power to all the abandoned buildings. Behind me were the glass jars filled with colorful candies they kept out of reach of us kids, who would gawk at them from the other side of the counter. The jars were still there, with their metal lids, but there wasn't a single candy left; seeing them like that, cold and transparent, they looked more like surgical supplies, a set of containers for the fruits of strange experiments.

The light barely reached back there. I decided to return later with a flashlight, but first I ran my hand along a couple of empty shelves, dragging my fingers through a layer of dust as rough as an animal's fur. On the top shelf, just when I couldn't reach any further, my hand bumped against something. I stood on tiptoe and carefully felt around. Cans. Cans stacked in squat little piles. I picked one up and slowly traced the paper label and pull tab with my finger. I brought it down from the shelf but couldn't read the label. It wasn't until I was standing in the trickle of light from the broken door that I was able to see the drawing and blue letters: *Tuna in oil*. My god. For a moment, that was all I could think: *My god*. I was euphoric, almost dizzy; I couldn't remember the last time I'd seen one of those. I went back to the display and stepped on the bottom shelf so I could reach all the way back. Eleven cans, forgotten all the way against the wall on that top shelf. I brought them down and shoved a few into my pockets and the rest into my scarf, tying them up like a package.

I left through the same hole I came in, but I wasn't as agile this time. My pant leg caught on a splinter and tore a little. The adrenaline felt like fire, like a foreign substance coursing through my body. Impossible to wait until I got home. I sat on the curb and wiped one of the cans with my sleeve. It didn't sparkle like a treasure chest, but that's what it felt like. Inside was the impossible, the forbidden flesh of an extinct animal. Its distant cousins, unknown mutations, swam in our river. No one bothered them; without natural predators the mutations proliferated, and the time would come, if it hadn't already, when they would be the only creatures left in the sea.

I pulled the tab. A marine scent rose immediately from the open can. I breathed in and brought the pink flesh to my nose with my eyes half-closed, shot back into memory like a bullet. Fast, painful. I saw the women in their white coveralls gripping the knives they used for scaling the freshly caught fish in San Felipe's port—the slippery white floor, the nauseating odor. That same knife would be used for gutting: it would open a long fissure in the creature and a gloved hand would reach in to shovel out organs and liquids.

My hands were filthy, completely black with dust, but I used my fingers like pincers to grab a piece of tuna and stick it in my mouth. I didn't look at the expiration date on the can. It didn't matter; I know I would have eaten whatever was inside, even if it had fossilized. I pressed my tongue against the roof of my mouth, releasing the oil. The bullet bored deeper into my memory and I couldn't tell anymore if what I was biting into was a piece of fruit, a peach that loosed a syrupy juice I had to lick from between my fingers before it ran all the way down my arm, or if what I was hearing were flies buzzing around pears that had bruised in places that were like patches of softer skin, or if I was watching Delfa patiently remove the seeds from a watermelon, digging around the crunchy, porous red pulp. Delfa and the smell of candied nuts, a scent that mingled with the odor of bleach and chamomile soap. All the smells in the world fit in Delfa's hands. The oil trickled between my fingers, down my palm, over my wrist, and into the sleeve of my coat. My chin was slippery and smooth. I tried to wipe my face clean, but I just ended up spreading the oil and the smell of fish around. I figured that the soot from my fingers must have spread all over, too, and I liked picturing myself in a kind of ritual face paint, my own oily black marks like a declaration of war. If there was an animal beside the cockroaches left in this city, it would have been drawn to me. I rose from the curb, feeling the grease on my hands and the company of the fog, its power, and turned to walk home.

What is silence?
The pause between one thought and the next.

That night I made rice with tuna and mayonnaise. What I wouldn't have given for a tomato, even one of those hydroponic ones grown in incubators, a tomato plump from injections of water or fungicides, a tomato with no flavor at all but which at least evoked the idea of a tomato. I served our meal on big plates with gilded edges and flowers with long, graceful stems instead of the small, chipped ones we usually used. It was a feast, but Mauro couldn't tell. We sat on the floor with our plates on the coffee table, in front of the television. There was an ad on for frozen hamburgers. The round bun, the steaming, melted cheese, and a halo of salt particles that had leapt sparkling into the air, held aloft by the magic of slow motion. A bite taken out of the burger revealed the fresh, juicy red meat in the center—nothing like the dry, flat patties as hard as a rubber sole that actually came in the box. Mauro's parents always included them in the month's supplies, and they were the first thing to run out. On the box was the cartoon of a cow grazing on a beautiful hill, underneath the red logo of the national processing plant. I turned off the television and Mauro whined.

'No,' he said. 'Yes TV.'

'We're going to eat something special.'

It was the first time I didn't want to distract him from food, but he made a face as he took a bite. The taste was too strong for him maybe, too unfamiliar for his youthful taste buds. He stirred the rice around with his spoon and studied the shredded tuna. His hesitation lasted one more second before he gathered a heap of rice and swallowed it without chewing.

'Slow down,' I said.

'Hungry,' he whined again.

'You're eating, Mauro, you can't be hungry.'

'Where's the moon?'

'There's fog today. Do you want to see if you can find it?'

He shook his head. Without the wind or the television, the only sound was his spoon scraping across the plate.

'Today is a happy day,' I said.

He flashed me his laden cheeks and teeth white with mayonnaise. I watched him make an effort to chew ten times before swallowing, the way I'd shown him. The syndrome felt distant, defeated.

'Do you like it?'

The stuffed mouth murmured yes.

'We're going to be okay,' I said. 'I promise.'

The next morning I woke up feeling that joyful sense of impatience, the anticipation that keeps you up half the night waiting for the dawn. The morning news was covering the only possible story: the fire at the processing plant, the dead animals and destroyed machines. The millions lost by foreign investors, breeders, the agronomist. I wondered if Mauro's parents had invested in the new plant, too. We all lose, they were saying on television, but I knew better.

Some people lost, and others bounced back. For a moment, I imagined Mauro's father speaking into the camera like the host of *Dare to Dream*: Dreams are only dreams . . . but here they become reality.

The weather forecast scrolled across the bottom of the screen: *Fog and cold temperatures, low risk of wind.*

'Is today a happy day?' asked Mauro. He was playing on the floor, ignoring the news.

'It is,' I said.

I went to the kitchen and squeezed soap on our breakfast dishes, then I got Mauro's clothes ready the way I did when they came to get him, making something like a rag doll on the bed.

'To the bath with you,' I said, and he followed me, resigned.

I bathed him well. I had to run my soapy finger along the folds of his abdomen, where black lines of dried sweat and grime accumulated. His flesh offered no resistance. It seemed endless, without organs. I dried him off brusquely, to warm him up; he whined and made the job difficult, but in the end he lifted his arms so I could put his favorite shirt on him. While I helped him with his socks and shoes, I asked him to find the sun and tell me where it was. He looked out the window, searching for the point of light behind ring after ring of dense clouds. I combed his hair to the side—not with my fingers like always but making a nice straight part with a fine-tooth comb—then I asked him to lift his arms again so I could put on his polar fleece. It matched his red hat and gloves—one of the first useless gifts from his mother, because it was too risky to take Mauro outside, and because she herself had forbidden it. He was finally getting the chance to wear them; in all that red, he looked like a merry link of chorizo.

'Did you find it?' I asked.

He pointed to the top right corner of the window, behind the television. I turned and there it was, that pale gleam.

'Very good!'

'Are we going to see horses?' he asked.

'No, we're going to see my mom.'

'My mom.'

'No, mine. Are you happy?'

His double chin rubbed against the collar of his thermal fleece as he nodded, smiling at me, his eyes squinted into little slits.

He was too hot in his clothes; I watched him struggle with his hat.

'Don't take any of that off, we're about to leave,' I said.

I finished putting on my coat, and while Mauro waited for me in the doorway, taking in the cold air of the hall, I went into my room, opened the safe, and took out three cans of tuna. I stuck them in my coat pocket; I didn't want them in my backpack with the books, where they might be stolen.

'Don't move,' I said. 'Can you count to ten for me?'

I heard him counting: One, two, three, four.

I closed the safe, hid the key, and put my backpack on.

'Ready.' I bent down to give him a kiss on the forehead, but it landed next to his eye. He wiped the spot with the back of his hand.

'You're wiping it away? How about you give me one, then?'

'Okay,' he said.

He gave me a tepid kiss on the cheek, and we didn't say anything more for a while. We walked down the stairs and into the plaza, thick with clouds and silence. He squeezed my hand, even though it would have been impossible to lose him, dressed all in red from the waist up, big and round in a textureless landscape.

We crossed the plaza diagonally. I figured we would have a better chance of finding a car along the rambla closer to the port. Mauro wanted to get on the swings, but I didn't let him. I allowed him to run a little, his arms stiff in all his layers, as long as he stayed on the gravel path. I felt bad denying him; I remember asking my mother permission to go to the rocks in San Felipe, or to the restaurant where the divers went. No, she'd say, and I'd hate her. No, Mauro, *no*. Just like that, it had become my catchphrase.

'No,' I said again, when he insisted about the swings, rusted and barely moving over a mud pit no one had set foot on in ages. 'We have to go.'

We got into the second taxi that stopped for us. I didn't trust the first driver, but this one had been a professional and was quick to show me his union card—long expired, but complete with logo and watermark. As soon as he started the engine, the driver tried to get a conversation going. He was the chatty type, one of those who begin every sentence with 'what if I told you that . . .' and then immediately tell you.

'What was I going to do, stare at the ceiling all day?' he said. 'A few drivers got assigned to politicians, but most of us they just sent home. To wait. Because the union couldn't be responsible for the health risks.'

'And they couldn't send you inland?'

'Everything costs a fortune there. Go inland, how? Sure, they'll assign you, but you gotta pay your own way, soup to nuts.'

Mauro was silent, staring out the window. He was sucking his index finger, chewing on it.

'What's our friend here called?' the man asked.

'Mauro,' I said.

'How old are you, Mauro?'

He didn't take his eyes off the window; I don't even think he heard the question.

'He's really focused,' I said by way of an apology.

'There are chatty people, and there are focused people,' said the man. 'I had a cousin—well, I guess I still do, even if I haven't heard a thing from her in twenty years—went on a trip to India. Dentist and all, my cousin Estela. Nothing real special about her, but no dummy, neither. Well, what if I told you she went over there and met a Sister, a nun, and just up and decided she wasn't coming back.' He paused, enjoying the suspense he'd managed to create. 'Spent a whole year sleeping on a wooden board. I don't remember what the group was called now, Sisters of Silence or whatnot, something to do with Mother Teresa. Anyway, Estelita, that's what we used to call her, left everything behind and stayed over there. Only came back once, to renew her passport. She'd lost all her teeth. Life's ironic, isn't it? That was the last time we heard anything from her. After that she took a vow of silence and never spoke again. Can you imagine? Never spoke again. Her mother died and she didn't even bother coming back. Her heart had turned to stone.'

I paid five hundred pesos to get to Los Pozos, more than the old man had charged me the last time I went to see my mother, and five times more than the official taxis charged in the old days. That's how things were now. Everything changes like the ocean currents. That's how it was with Max. We both changed constantly, except we called it 'growing' and thought it would stop at some point. When? Soon, when we're not young anymore, when we're finally as calm as two fossils.

My mother's street was covered in leaves; we heard them crackle under the tires as the car turned her corner and slowed to drop us in front of her house. The aftermath of the last wind, except the residents used to sweep them up into piles and burn them. That's the smell I associate with Los Pozos and other tree-lined neighborhoods. Not like the port, which smelled like fumes coming off the river and the fishing boats. But it seemed no one in Los Pozos was taking care of the leaves anymore, and Mauro started kicking them as soon as he got out of the taxi. The leaves fluttered like confetti and fell back to the ground around him. He stretched out his arms, trying to catch them. It was like rain, only dry, and it sparked a surge of joy in me as well. The car drove away in reverse because the street was a dead end. Dark tire tracks running parallel on one side of the road; on the other, a giant pillow of leaves.

'Follow me!' I called to Mauro, heading several feet into the virgin territory. 'Look! They crunch!'

He walked over to where I stood, stepping down hard, releasing his colossal weight onto one foot too small for his size, then the other. I crouched, grabbed an armful of leaves, and threw them into the air. Mauro started kicking again, but when he saw that his leaves weren't flying as high as mine, he began to copy me.

'It's raining!' I said, and he laughed.

'Raining!' he repeated, and before the last leaf touched the ground he was already reaching for more. The layers underneath smelled of damp and rot, but I didn't care.

'Mom!' I called, because there was no way in all this silence that my mother hadn't heard the car door or our laughter under her window. 'Mom!'

But she didn't come outside and she wasn't going to. No one in the neighborhood poked their head out. A moment of anger followed— frustration, the usual reproaches: she can't even be bothered to come to the door, I'll make damn sure she hears me out here, and other variations on bitterness. Then I grabbed Mauro's leaf-flecked hand, walked him up to the door, knocked two or three times, and tried to look through the window (Mauro made a visor with his hands against the glass), but we couldn't see anything. She wasn't in the garden, either. Her gardening basket was on the wrought iron table with her gloves inside it; they were covered in dirt, as always. Her plants were neat and healthy, free of pests, but the hibiscus and Cape jasmine weren't flowering. Mauro wandered through the bushes while I climbed the three steps to the kitchen door and tried the knob. It was unlocked.

I will never see her again, as I said, and I'll conjure a thousand and one times like a ghost the image of her motionless figure behind the voile curtain, my kiss sliding off the oily skin of her forehead, the smell of her unwashed hair, also oily, and the roughness of her robe, which seemed like it was made from a quilt. I'll search the whole house but won't find a single sign of life, or death. Kitchen cabinets empty, except for a bag of lentils tied with a knot and several untouched cups of Meatrite in the refrigerator. A layer of dust on the shelves. Through the kitchen window I will see Mauro standing on the hard earth of the flower beds with my mother's basket hanging from one arm, picking her sacred stems and seedlings. I will call to her a few times like a frightened child and will realize I'm shouting 'Leonor,' not 'Mom,' and that I haven't called her by her given name since Delfa was alive and was my real mother. I won't find anything: no phone number, no address, no note. Through the window that looks onto the street I'll see the schoolteacher's house with the shutters down and will know right away that she is gone. The most ridiculous part of all this will be the gesture of removing the books from my backpack and stacking them on the table. Carefully, as if my mother were watching. All those books I borrowed and returned unread. All those times my heart raced when she asked me a question about this or that story. And yet.

I won't leave right away. I'll sit for a while longer on the high-backed couch where once I thought I'd found her dead, the fog draped over her like a shroud. Mauro will come inside with the basket full of buds, plants pulled out by the roots, and dry leaves. He'll sit close to me and pour some of the basket's contents onto the Persian rug. If she thinks I'm going to go looking for her, I'll mutter like a broken record. If she thinks I'm going to track her through all those inland cities . . . Not once will I consider that she might be at Clinics, bedridden. Mauro will pile his bounty on top of my feet, as if he were burying them, and I will let him be as he arranges flowers, leaves, and a handful of dirt on my shoes.

'Dirty,' he'll say, wiping his hands on the carpet.

'It's okay. We're going now.'

I know that at some point I stood, destroying his floral arrangement. I needed to find a private cab in that dying neighborhood before the alarm sounded. Mauro said he didn't want to go, and I told him he could take the basket.

We walked a long way before reaching an avenue that showed signs of human activity. I was dragging Mauro behind me, squeezing his hand so hard it had probably gone numb. He tried to wriggle free. Stay with me, I said. My other hand was wrapped around the basket he'd gotten tired of carrying. We passed a small neo-Gothic church with its doors closed. When I was a little girl, I'd dreamed of getting married in that church. Of course, when Max and I finally did get married, we only had a civil ceremony. My mother was against the union even though she'd known Max his whole life, or maybe because she'd known him his whole life. You're digging your own grave, she'd said, but for me it was the other way around—I felt like Max was saving me from the grave I had been lying in my whole life. A few weeks before the ceremony, my mother informed me that she had an important business trip coming up. I won't be able to make it to your wedding, she said. I gave her a piece of my mind and we didn't talk for two weeks, during which I swore I never wanted to see her again. In the end, she canceled her trip, and they sent in her place a blonde who'd just started working at the company—a woman who, according to my mother, had the demeanor of a drowsy horse. She was perfectly nice to everyone at the ceremony and the toast, but a few days later we heard that the blonde hadn't managed to land the client. She was fired not long after that. What could we expect from a drowsy horse, my mother shook her head sadly, I sent that poor creature to the slaughterhouse. But she made it perfectly clear that the one who'd sent the woman to the slaughterhouse was me.

When we got into the taxi (a real yellow cab turned into a medical transport vehicle, which picked up private fares behind the union's back), I asked the driver if he knew of any underground markets. He said there was one out in Puente Arena and more often than not a few vendors set up shop in the tunnel in Siete Caminos.

'They come and go,' he said. 'One minute they've got folding tables set up and everything, and the next, poof. Vanished.'

'Maybe they're ghosts.'

The driver laughed.

'Maybe we're all ghosts,' I added.

'I don't think so,' he replied, shaking his head. 'I don't think ghosts get hungry. I'll tell you what, though, they won't sell you so much as a crust of bread for less than two hundred pesos.'

'Seems like ghosts have a mind for business.'

'I'd take you,' said the driver, 'but all the roads around Siete Caminos are closed.'

'Why's that?'

'You didn't hear? A woman jumped off a building. She had a little boy just the same age as yours.'

Mauro didn't look up; he was playing and had dug his hands deep into the dirt in his basket. He was muttering something, a story he'd made up that kept him far from us.

'Looks like the wind drove her crazy. Before she jumped, she tore off all her clothes.'

'What'll happen to the boy?'

'No,' said the man, meeting my gaze in the rearview mirror. 'She took him with her.'

I turned on the television as soon as we got home. Sure enough, the announcers were talking about the woman who had jumped into the void with her child in her arms. Video footage captured by a drone had just shown a black dot falling from the ninth floor of a building. It was only two seconds long and had been taken from so far away, at such a low resolution, that it didn't manage to show anything human. If someone had turned on their television right then, they would have simply seen a bad pixel, a fly buzzing past. The news anchors took care of the rest. They said: *madness, unstable, out of control*. They said: *injustice, atrocity*, and *inalienable right*, as they ran and reran the image of the fly, which had been marked with a red circle so we could all identify it. When the cameras turned to the street, they showed an area cordoned off with the same yellow tape they'd used to close the beaches, and a swarm of police officers in German respirator masks. The bodies lay on the sidewalk covered with plastic bags.

Everything has an edge: even the ocean is contained by continents.

Is an edge the border of itself?

An edge is the beginning of another edge.

So what's the edge of distance?

The closest point between two things.

And of the mind?

Forgetting.

I threw the doors to my bedroom closets open. I felt around the top shelves, where I kept extra pillows and blankets wrapped in plastic, and pulled down my black bag. I tossed it on the bed and began to pile shirts, pants, and sweaters around it. Mauro poked his head through the doorway, basket in hand.

'Horses?'

'Yes,' I said. 'We're going on a trip.'

He walked over to me and rested the dirty basket on my bed.

'Go stand over there, Mauro. Let me pack this bag.'

He hadn't even taken off his polar fleece yet, but I didn't realize that until much later. I was making piles at top speed: passport, money, a nearly blank notebook with a few telephone numbers and addresses jotted down in it. From Mauro's room I grabbed socks and underwear, his lace-up shoes, his raincoat. I scurried back and forth, building a mound of clothing too high for the long black bag, with all its zippers and hidden compartments. Little by little the idea took shape, and I threw everything that wasn't essential on the floor: clothing, toys, toiletries, objects with no purpose other than to evoke memories. What can we expect to see next? I heard someone on television ask. The story of the woman who had jumped from the building had already been discarded and they were talking about the fire again, the loss of livestock. What's the prognosis?

I must have spent two or three hours on that task, though time was measured by a different kind of clock in those days: wind or fog, gray or red, power or blackout; it passed according to Mauro's cycles of hunger, the preparation of meals, and my ability to keep my distance from Max. Each bomb had its own unique ticking. So when I talk about days, weeks, and hours, I do it as a way to organize my thoughts, to give meaning to a stagnant memory.

Even so, there was a moment when everything sped up.

Like a tear in a piece of fabric pulled tight. As if the fog opened for the briefest moment to reveal its insides, made of a different time and substance. First, I thought I heard someone knocking on the door. Knocking? Or a single knock? The acoustic mirage caught me so off guard I thought of my mother. This would be typical of her, I thought, doing things this way to keep us all on tenterhooks. Over the years, I'd come to see my mother as one extended cliché and couldn't talk about her without using idioms my editor would have immediately crossed out: *pearls before swine, tenterhooks, don't let the door hit you on the way out.* The bag sat open on the bed, relatively light and still empty in the corners where socks and shoes would go. Mauro had tugged off his hat and polar fleece and was playing on the floor in the middle of piles of dirt, arranging stems and leaves into a strange ikebana. I was walking in circles around the apartment. A single moment of stillness could derail me and I knew it, so I forced myself to fold clothes, open and close drawers, check hiding places, and probe forgotten corners. A moment earlier, I'd asked Mauro to change the channel and he'd grabbed the remote and started pressing buttons until we found a special on the woman who had jumped from the building. Now they were interviewing an old neighbor of hers. She was pretty reserved, the man said, hard to read. Then the knocking started again. Yes, definitely, there it was: firm, insistent. Mauro and I jumped. We looked at the door. What did we do next? I know that Mauro got scared and ran to hide in his room. I waited a moment, thinking of my mother and feeling my rage vibrate like a chord inside me, but I finished what I was doing, forcing myself to calm down. Then I went to the door and pressed my eye to the peephole, a convex lens that reminded me of those old plastic cones that used to have a tiny photo at one end. The picture always looked so distant and ghostly, illuminated from behind by whatever light source you held the cone up to. You had to close one eye to the outside world and open the other to the world inside that lit space. The peephole was dirty, there was a piece of lint trapped between the two layers of glass, so all I could make out was a figure standing too close to the door; a figure that didn't seem to belong to a police officer, at least.

I opened the door and there—in her impeccable gray business suit, in the cold hallway of my abandoned building—stood Mauro's mother. But my stubborn mind, which latches on to things so tenaciously, was still on *my* mother; I thought that maybe this woman came with news, that they'd met inland at some ridiculous book club meeting accompanied by piano music. Finally, I thought, you finally got what you wanted.

'I'm sorry,' she said. 'The phone lines have been down.'

And that's when I noticed that she didn't have any boxes of food with her. It was just her, a woman barely five feet tall, in her little mouse-gray suit with a blue handkerchief tied around her neck. It was impossible to imagine Mauro coming out of that tiny body, so perfectly arrogant in its angular slightness. I invited her in, but she declined. She preferred to stay clear of the slovenliness, the stale air, the food-stained couch sunken in the middle, the pots crusted with rice and garbanzos. She preferred a tidier handoff.

'I had no way of letting you know,' she said.

I turned back toward the apartment, my hand still on the doorknob.

'Look who's here!' I called, and my voice didn't waver. 'Mauro, come see.'

But he didn't come out, and the two of us stood in silence, taking measure of one another, waiting for the sound of his footsteps or some kind of sign from him, and right now as I say this . . . as I say this I'm reminded of that little fish that soared through the air on the fisherman's line, barely flicking its tail, offering us its silvery gleam, its tiny life.

A lack of air.

'I didn't get his clothes ready,' I said. 'If I had known . . .'

She attempted a smile. She didn't care. She'd buy him new clothes, she'd buy her little syndrome whatever he asked for, even food; when I started toward his room, she stopped me and told me not to pack anything since they didn't have much time. She spoke quickly, at the speed a body her size would speak, lacking the weight necessary to hold air inside.

'The fog is thick,' I said, and immediately felt ridiculous, like an old seaman navigating by the moon and the constellations. I must have looked like one, too. The woman must have thought: Look at what all this has done to her. Or maybe just: She had it coming.

'We didn't have any food,' I said. 'We had nothing.'

'I'm sorry, there were so many things to get in order. There were no phone lines, it wasn't possible.'

Then she remembered something. She patted her pockets. She took two steps forward on the dirty industrial carpeting and held the envelope out to me. I reached for it like a robot, like one of those cash machines that suck deposits in through a slot, and noticed that it was thicker than usual.

'We really appreciate everything you've done for Mauro,' she said. 'Both my husband and I. Really.'

'But he's not ready,' I said. 'I wasn't expecting you.'

The woman sighed, and for a second I thought she was going to rest her hand on mine.

'Listen. He doesn't think about me, or you. He only thinks about his next meal.'

Mauro poked his head out of his room: thick, tangled hair and small eyes squinting to focus.

'Who's this here?' I asked, unable to answer the question myself. He poked his head a little further out, followed by a leg, then a shoulder and an arm, and he saw her. He was dressed, but didn't have his shoes on. 'Get your shoes on, hurry,' I said, but that exhaustion had returned, that brutal exhaustion. I was sick and tired of giving him orders, of being a rule dispenser. I wanted us to play together, to jump down the stairs two at a time while holding hands; I wanted to play hide-and-seek in the fog and sit on the motionless swings. Mauro said no, no, he didn't want to go. His hands were covered in dirt, his black fingers pressed against the wall. The woman, meanwhile, was shifting her weight from one foot to the other. The cold had passed through her nice little suit and she was shivering.

'Tell him we don't have time for this,' she ordered, though Mauro was right in front of her, too.

'You heard your mother,' I said. Right then I finally let go of the doorknob. Was there still time? Yes, we were still here, together, nowhere else. The doorknob had warmed under my hand, and I felt a shock of cold air against my palm. I walked over to Mauro, took him by the arm, and led him to the sofa. He sat with his legs dangling; he didn't reach the carpet. I brought his shoes over and opened the laces wide. I didn't want to struggle with him, to ask him to help me and be forced to scold him: Help a little, Mauro, push your foot in. I didn't want that woman to see my anguish and take pity on me. I didn't want any kind of bond forming between us. I put Mauro's shoes on, without socks. He was going to get cold. The rough seams must have been chafing his feet. I squeezed his instep, a gentle pressure to comfort him, to communicate to him that he was ready.

'You're going to visit the horses,' I said. 'You like that.'

'No,' he said. 'Don't like.'

'What do you mean you don't like it?' I took his dirty hand in mine and kissed the moist hollow of his palm. 'Of course you do.'

Then Mauro will go. He will be crying. He will walk grudgingly, in front of me, to the door.

'Say goodbye, Mauro,' the woman will say. 'Say a nice goodbye.'

He will hug me, hanging from my legs, and I will need to hold on to the door to keep my balance. She will say his name several times.

Mauro, she will say, Mauro. She will try to hide her exasperation. I will see the hatred in her eyes. She will know that I'm not helping, that I'm not giving the orders that work or offering effective, merciful lies. She will peel one of Mauro's hands from my leg and he'll let her, docile, but he won't release the other, which I will feel wrap tighter and squeeze like a snake. I will let myself be strangled, will not resist the pressure of his arm. The woman will tug on Mauro's free hand, then tug harder, hating me more than ever, until he finally loses his grip and flies backward with a shriek. *Naaaaaa, naaaaa.* Mauro will drop to the floor and she will need to drag his soft bulk across the carpet, scratching and burning his skin. I will think how much that must hurt, but I will not move.

Before she leaves, the woman will turn toward me from where she stands by the staircase.

'I'm expecting,' she will say, without joy or enthusiasm.

I won't understand at first what she's expecting. What else could she possibly want from me? I will feel ashamed, thinking my face is covered in tears, but when I touch my cheeks, I will notice they are dry. I will only understand when she rests a hand low on her belly, still as tight and flat as a sheet. I won't know what to say, so I'll stand there silent, bobbing my head. Then I will tell them to drive safely.

I will say, 'He's like this because I didn't get him ready.'

Mauro will still be howling. I will see the disappointment in the woman's eyes, in the hand held against her belly as if to shield her new child from me.

'You should get out of here, you know,' she will say. 'Today. As soon as you . . .'

She won't finish her sentence, Mauro's hand dangling from hers like an extension of her body. As short as she is, she will look tall beside her sick child, beside the syndrome crumpled on the hallway carpet, face tucked in the crook of one arm as if he were taking a nap: a rock shaped like a human. From all the way up there, she will repeat Mauro's name, and it will sound like her property: now she is the only one who can say it, she is the only one who can grip that soft hand with brutal force and pull it, pull him, the whale boy, the dinosaur boy, down the stairs.

They paid me so that, when this day came, I would let him go.

Inside nothing, what is there?
Nothing.
And inside that nothing?
Infinity.

Trucks arrived and took everyone away. Mauro's mother had known something, I realized; I also realized that she couldn't tell me what she knew. How powerful *were* his parents? People were being brought to relocation camps, the technical name for a place that had nothing to do with bonfires and guitar circles. At least that's what they said on television; what I saw was canvas-top military trucks parked on street corners and thin lines of people filing out of buildings. They looked defeated, ashamed of having bought into a fantasy. The power went out several times that weekend, but it always returned with the same images: people emerging from the most unlikely places like dazed mice, climbing into the trucks empty-handed or with suitcases they were told to leave on the sidewalk. They walked with their heads bowed, like schoolchildren who'd gotten into trouble and knew it. That's what you get, little ones: don't do the crime if you can't do the time. They'll learn. They're mischievous, dim-witted. They'll learn and all this will be left in the past, a bad memory. They will climb into the trucks cold, hungry, covered in fleas and lice, teeth shattered and stomachs turned from eating plaster and dry seeds. They will climb gratefully into the trucks. And the State will need no payment other than this gratitude.

The evacuation lasted two days and two nights. No one would have guessed there were so many people left. The television didn't show the ones who resisted, but I could imagine what happened to them, how they were dragged, how their clothes were pulled off, how they were handcuffed and shoved into trucks. One time they did show a blockade in Barrio Alto that was handled without major incident: no projectiles or homemade grenades, just a few remarkably gaunt residents barricaded behind sheets of corrugated metal.

The police patrolled the streets and searched inside buildings for survivors. On Sunday afternoon, I heard them in mine. They were making a racket, shouting orders to one another, rattling door-knobs, banging their nightsticks on every door. I stayed very still, sitting on the couch with the television off, and listened to them move along my hallway.

'Five-oh-one!' they shouted. 'Five-oh-two! Five-oh-three!'

I imagined that one of the policemen probably carried a list of the apartments that had already been inspected, a lanky bureaucrat not particularly skilled at violence who was charged with putting a check mark next to each number on his list. I prepared myself. I knew they were going to knock and didn't want to be startled. The nightstick crashed against my door. *Bam, bam, bam.* Just three times but with brute force, like they were trying to break it down.

'Police. Evacuation,' yelled one. I heard him jiggle the knob. Then a fist pounded on the door, but they didn't try to force their way in. They would later, of course, when the news cameras had moved on to other places and other stories; they'd knock down every door in the city and take everything that could still be sold.

'Police!' They knocked again.

I didn't move. My nerves were shot, but I managed to stay still. My heart was beating so fast it felt like I'd swallowed a humming-bird. There was a time when I was proud of knowing this sort of thing: a hummingbird beats its wings more than fifty-five times each second, generating lift on both the forward and backward strokes. It's how they hover in the air, motionless to the naked eye. That was me—motionless to the naked eye as they continued along the hall and then headed upstairs.

It wasn't until I heard the trucks pull away, leaving the port sub-merged in silence, that I dared to stand up. I looked out the window. Nothing seemed to have changed, and yet the fog looked harder, more compact, as if it had closed in on me. I lowered the blinds and turned on the television. On the news, they were talking about re-locating the hospital. Where were they taking it? Some inland city, but they wouldn't say which. To avoid riots and more protests. They were broadcasting live. You could see the patients being rolled into the giant elevators at Clinics in wheelchairs, or on gurneys with in-travenous drips and oxygen masks. No one living inland wanted their hypersanitized cities overrun by the infected; no one wanted to risk them shedding their skin like a dirty robe, letting it fall to the fertile ground so full of life. So what were they going to do with them? What were they going to do with Max? I was glued to the television because something told me I would see him among the infected and the doctors running this way and that. But in my fantasy I pictured him in a fine black suit, like a singer from another era; he walked out of Clinics on his own two feet with that crooked half smile on his face, then looked straight into the camera, straight at me, and reached out his hand ceremoniously as if he were asking me to dance.

'So you're leaving, too?'

But he didn't answer; he couldn't hear me. He just stayed like that, with his hand reaching toward me, a large hand as flat as a eucalyptus leaf, a dark hand that opened but offered nothing, like the hands of a magician. Who wants a rabbit? Who wants a flower? What we want is a nice roasted chicken, a potato grown in the earth, a strawberry that doesn't taste like tap water.

My mother once told me that Max had given me nothing but the certainty of loss. She wasn't entirely wrong, but absence wasn't nothing. Sometimes it was everything. Absence was a thing solid enough to cling to; solid enough, even, to be the foundation on which to build a life.

I went back to my room and took the money out of my black bag. The small bills were in a white envelope, the big ones were in a black trash bag, sealed with tape. Night had fallen; after turning off the television I raised the blinds one by one. They crackled like lightning. In the distance, you could see the lights on the cranes and sense the bulk of the shipping containers. I opened a window and immediately recognized the smell of the port, a combination of algae and spilled gasoline. That smell was mine, just like that money was mine. I pulled the bills from the envelope. I didn't count them; there was no need to count what no one would take from me. I looked at the lights in that machine graveyard and they looked back at me— cyclopic, pitiful, expectant—one light at the top of each crane, for what? Maybe so the State helicopters wouldn't end up skewered on them. I released a bill and it floated downward slowly, almost refusing to fall into the thick mesh of the night. Then another, and another. At least the laws of physics hadn't changed. Who would have thought they could bring such comfort? Those small immutable things; incomprehensible, but immutable. The bills fell, scraping the fog, and I returned to the sofa and nodded off for a few hours, deaf from the silence. Every now and then I jumped at the sound of my own breathing, the sensation of my legs rubbing against one another. At some point, the power went out for good.

It was like waiting for something for a long time. But what was I waiting for? Sometimes I think ridiculous thoughts. What color is silence? I could ask the pundits on television. White, they'd say, as if your head were wrapped in cotton. Black, they'd say, like death itself. But there's nothing especially dramatic about silence. If it were a color it would be gray like the fog, which is neither solid nor liquid, neither opaque nor transparent, but still manages to wipe out everything in its path. And Mauro is red. A red splotch in a garden. An interior landscape.

I can't stop thinking about the way his mother had scowled at me after she told me she was expecting. What did her body know that she didn't? The same hand that had rested gently on her belly later dragged Mauro down the hall; she tugged on his arm, but her fingers couldn't close around the soft circumference of his wrist. I keep seeing her expression when she turned to look at me from the stairs, a tightness not only around her mouth, but across her whole face. She had looked at me as if I were an island and she were a shipwrecked sailor being pulled out to sea.

Can you imagine the space between your eyes?

Can you imagine the space filled by your tongue?

Can you imagine the space held by the roof of your mouth,
your gums, your teeth?

Can you imagine the space behind your eyes?

Can you imagine the space filled by your head, your brain,
your mouth, the throat that swells to fill your neck?

Can you imagine the distance between your shoulders and
your elbows?

Can you imagine the distance between your elbow and your wrist,
the space filled by your forearm?

Can you imagine the space filled by your fingers, including the
space between your flesh and your bones?

Can you imagine the space filled by your chest, the space inside
your lungs?

Can you imagine the space between your clavicle and your spine,
the distance between your kneecap and your foot?

Can you imagine the space filled by your entire body, all at once?

Can you imagine that space expanding beyond you, extending
forward indefinitely?

Can you imagine the space that expands beneath you, through
the earth and on and on forever, to the other side of the stars?

Can you imagine the space filled by your body and the infinite
space that spreads outward forever, in all directions,
a continuous space?

Can you imagine the space filling your stomach?

In a kidney transplant, the diseased organ is replaced by a healthy one. The new organ might be the product of a supreme act of generosity or a string of bureaucratic coincidences. Could anyone tell the difference? The surgeon? The medical examiner? Does the healthy organ bear the mark of its origin, some trace of sacrifice? The new kidney sometimes takes a while to start working; this period is called delayed graft function. I think about this period of suspended time, when the old no longer works and the new refuses to replace it.

Mauro's body will continue to grow, but the rest will stay the same, lost forever in his Legos and his animal books. He will learn new words, different games. But how long will his memory of me last? Will he feel like something's missing, even something very small, the way someone might run their tongue over the hole left when a tooth falls out?

I had another lucid dream the last night I spent at home: I saw animals walking into an enormous black box, like the kind magicians use for sawing their assistants in half. There were cows and pigs and chickens; horses, capybaras, and mules. The animals entered the box and immediately fell through a trapdoor, a kind of false floor that cast them into a pit the size of the ocean. There was an altar down there made of dead birds and bags of trash, and people knelt before it making an offering of something, I couldn't quite see what, something that looked like sand but whiter and more brilliant. They let the dazzling powder sift through their fingers onto the base of the altar as more animals rained down through the trapdoor.

I slept badly, always watching myself dream, and got up from the couch before sunrise. A thread of saliva and blood had trickled from my mouth, staining the gray fabric. I left the building around six. I had nothing in my backpack but my documents and the remaining cans of tuna. I had no destination or plan, either. The feeble dawn found me sitting on a concrete bench on the rambla. That pale light didn't fill gradually with sounds, as it had in another time; it simply revealed a few outlines: the port authority, the Masonic temple, the metal structure of the old gas tank, and the pier jutting out like a tongue in a diseased mouth. Then I was able to make out the colors of the water, the red sections, little islands of algae gently rocked by the river's breath. The dampness scaled the rocks. I could feel the fog clinging to me as if I were a statue and it were the moss that would eventually consume me. The sun tried to break through. It would fail. It would remain distant, faint, lost behind rings and rings of clouds.

I took a can of tuna from my backpack, pulled the tab on its lid, and ate its contents with my fingers. My hunger was an ache deep in my head and my bones that had silenced every other thought. When I finished slurping up the oil, I threw the can into the river, which was as calm as a pond, its murky reddish foam lining the base of the seawall. The can floated for a moment until the water found its way in and dragged it to the bottom. I opened another. I chewed and swallowed, but it was Mauro eating, not me. Mauro swallowed and his stomach was grateful for a second before demanding more. I slurped up the oil again and felt it trickle down my throat, giving me a bit of life. I licked the lid, which curled back onto itself, exploring its dangerous edge with my tongue. Max had once used that ring of sharp metal to slice the skin of his arms. He still had the white scars, if you looked carefully. He did it one afternoon when I was working at the agency, the only time during the week I dared to leave him alone, after hiding our knives and razor blades. Later, in one of those bitter arguments before the divorce, I threw in his face that I'd taken care of him in his darkest days. I screamed it at him. He shot back, also screaming, that surveillance was not the same thing as care.

The second can sank more quickly than the first. I pictured it slowly descending and coming to rest on the trash that carpeted the bottom. The river absorbed it without bubbles or concentric rings, and I searched in vain for a trace of the exact place where the can had broken the water. The fog clutched the air. I lay back on the bench, resting my head on my backpack, and was lulled to sleep by the sound of the water lapping like a cat at the seawall.

Where do forgotten hours go? Lost images? An image is the reproduction of an object by the light it reflects. But what light does an absence reflect? Writing it is useless; I should dream it, smash the pieces of the broken urn so that no one, not even me, can put it back together. For a second I feel like I'm speeding downhill on a bicycle, my knees lifted so my feet don't get caught in the whirling pedals. I feel the breeze on my face. And there's Delfa down below, arms open to catch me. But no, no one is there waiting, and the road stretches out long and full of mirages, asphalt humming under the sun.

I don't know when I open my eyes again. The fog presses down with its gray fist and not one trace of pink disturbs the sky. The smell of the algae is heavy and acidic, like a thousand pieces of fruit fermenting at once.

I stand.

I walk toward the hill: thin trails of smoke curl upward behind the cranes.

Hours will go by before I see the truck, an old Ford pickup brimming with scrap metal, broken furniture, and recyclable bottles. Beside it, a shadow. A broken silhouette: the top half of a body hidden inside a dumpster, the other half a counterweight keeping it safe.

I cannot stop a future that has already arrived.

Gradually, the image will fold in on itself. We will drive away slowly, the spectral glow of our headlights puncturing the night. And the city will be emptied like a body stripped of entrails, a cleaned carcass in the distance under a swirling will-o'-the-wisp.

about the author

Fernanda Trías, born in Uruguay in 1976, is the multi-award-winning author of three novels, of which *Pink Slime* is the second to be published in English. She is also the author of the short story collection *No soñarás flores* and the chapbook *El regreso*. Her work has been featured in anthologies in Germany, Colombia, Peru, Spain, Uruguay, the United States, and the United Kingdom, and has been translated into German, French, Hebrew, English, and Italian. She was awarded the National Uruguayan Literature Prize for her novel *La azotea* (*The Rooftop*). She lives in Bogotá, Colombia, where she has taught for several years at the Universidad Nacional's Creative Writing MFA program. In 2019 she was selected as Writer-in-Residence at the Universidad de los Andes, where she finished writing *Pink Slime*.

Heather Cleary is a translator and writer based in New York and Mexico City. She is the author of *The Translator's Visibility: Scenes from Contemporary Latin American Fiction*, about the power of translation to challenge norms of intellectual property and propriety; her other translations include *Witches* by Brenda Lozano, *Recital of the Dark Verses* by Luis Felipe Fabre, *Comemadre* by Roque Larraquy, *The Planets*, *The Dark*, and *The Incompletes* by Sergio Chejfec, and *Poems to Read on a Streetcar* by Oliverio Girondo. Cleary holds a PhD in Latin American and Iberian Cultures from Columbia University and teaches at Sarah Lawrence College.